Indebted

Sharon C. Cooper

ISBN: 978-1-946172-09-9
Paperback

Disclaimer
This story is a work of fiction. Names, characters, and
incidents are either products of the author's imagination or
are used fictitiously. Any resemblance to actual events,
locales, organizations or persons, living or dead, is entirely
coincidental.

Chapter One

Detective Lazarus Dimas had no tolerance for anyone who sold drugs—foot soldier or a drug lord—but he wanted to send thugs who beat up and stole from defenseless people to a special hell.

Scott Buckner, the wiry nineteen-year-old with blond hair and gray eyes stared back at him, defiance in his glare. The moron had been arrested three times for selling weed to kids and had now graduated to beating up and robbing old folks.

"Come on. Hit me back. I have no weapons on me and there are no cameras in here. You want to fight someone so bad, fight me. Here's your chance to take out all of your frustrations on someone else."

"I didn't do nothin'!"

"Then why yo' ass run when you saw us?" Laz balled his fists and put up his hands. "Now come on. Let's get this over with."

"Man, you're crazy! I already told you guys, I don't know what you're talking about." Scott slowly moved away from Laz, only to back into a wall. They were in an old warehouse that Laz used on occasion to distribute his own type of whoop-ass on young punks who needed a little fear beat into them.

"Do you hear this guy, Ashton?" Laz asked his partner who was standing a few feet away shaking his head. "Scott must not realize that we have video footage of some of his beating incidences."

It sickened Laz to watch the videos, but especially the most recent footage. Senseless. In each of the situations Scott could have taken the money without doing physical harm, but no. He either punched, kicked, and in the last occurrence, slammed an old man against the ATM. Laz planned to inflict the same pain on Scott as he'd done on his victims.

Laz punched him in the chest, and surprise registered on the kid's face. "What, you thought I was kidding? Come on, fight me back. This will be your one and only time to hit a cop and not get into trouble."

Scott glanced at Ashton.

"Go for it, man. Not too many people get a chance to knock Laz around. It's now or never."

"Oh, I get it. I hit you and you try to charge me with resisting arrest or some shit like that." Scott shook his head and tried sidestepping Laz. "No way. Not interested."

Laz popped him in the jaw. Not hard enough to break it, but hard enough to sting. Then he shot an uppercut to the kid's lip, drawing blood.

"Did you know the woman you attacked last week is someone's grandmother?" Laz punched him in the stomach and then in the face again, connecting with his nose.

"Man, you need to back up off of me," Scott seethed, wiping his bloody mouth and nose with the back of his sleeve. "I'm sorry, all right? I didn't mean to hurt them."

This only made Laz angrier. "What did you intend to do then, asshole? Did you think knocking them around didn't hurt?" He punched the kid again.

Scott hunched over holding his stomach. "I said I was sorry. I won't do it again," he croaked.

"Damn straight you won't do it again." Laz hit him two more times, sending him crumbling to the ground sobbing.

"All right, Laz. That's enough." Ashton pulled him off of

Scott.

"It's not enough until I know for sure he's not going to inflict pain on old people again. Who does that shit anyway?"

It was a rhetorical question, but Laz wished he could get answers on why some jerks did stupid stuff like that. He saw craziness more often than not on the streets of Atlanta, but stealing from the elderly? That was a new low.

That thought angered him all over again and he released a frustrated growl. "I should hit his ass again."

"Stop, man. I said I'm sorry," Scott groaned. "I'm sorry. Just arrest me already."

Ashton grunted and helped the kid up. "Now how are we supposed to take him in looking like this?"

Laz shrugged. "We handcuff his ass and then read him his rights."

"Well, I'm not writing this one up. This is all on you."

"Yeah, yeah, I know."

Laz and Detective Ashton Chambers had been partners for three years, and friends even longer. Ashton didn't agree with most of Laz's tactics, and didn't hesitate to call him out on his bullshit. Passionate about his job and getting as many criminals off the streets as possible, Laz was a *by-any-means-necessary* kind of guy. Since losing his long-time girlfriend nine years ago to violence, he had made it his mission to wipe the streets clean of as many miscreants as he could, especially drug dealers.

In Scott's case, there was still a chance to save him from the streets. Getting arrested over and over, and then released just as fast, hadn't taught the kid anything yet. Maybe now he'd think twice before beating up or stealing from anyone else.

While Ashton escorted Scott to the unmarked police car that Laz had parked inside the warehouse, Laz re-holstered his 9mm gun. He also pulled the gold police badge, hanging from a silver chain around his neck, out of the collar of his long-sleeve T-shirt and let it drop against his chest. Now he was ready.

Ashton shook his head, climbing into the passenger seat. "You know you got issues, right?"

"So I've been told."

This wouldn't go well with their sergeant, but Laz didn't care at the moment. The video of this guy punching a sixty-five-year-old grandmother over and over in her face, ignoring her cries, kept flashing through his mind.

Laz knew his actions weren't right, but he'd deal with the fallout when it happened.

*

"Laz! In my office. Now!" Sergeant Duane Ford's raspy, smoker's voice carried across the bullpen from his office door.

Laz tried not to groan, but one slipped out and he didn't miss the knowing glances and smirks coming from other detectives sitting at their desks nearby. He garnered a speech at least once every other week about his arrest procedures. As far as he was concerned, his actions in all of his cases were justified.

"Why does he always call me into his office and not both of us?" Laz asked Ashton, sitting at the desk facing his. "We're partners."

Ashton chuckled. "Because you always push the limits. One of these days, man…" Ashton didn't have to finish. Laz knew. His sergeant always went to bat for him, but there was going to come a time when Laz wouldn't be able to talk or negotiate his way out of the messes he willingly created.

"Go get your scolding and then hurry back. We need to follow up on that downtown store robbery."

Laz stood and shoved his cell phone into the front pocket of his jeans. "If I'm not out in ten minutes, come and interrupt."

A tingling started at the base of Laz's neck and crept higher. He didn't have to look around to know the cause because if that hadn't signaled him, the stirring in his gut would have. It never failed. Whenever the tall, leggy prosecutor was within thirty feet of him, whether he saw her or not, his body responded. Atlanta's assistant district attorney Journey Ramsey had an impact on him that he'd never experienced with another woman.

And there she was, as gorgeous as ever.

She followed a short distance behind another detective to one of the interrogation rooms. Her graceful, long stride enhanced her seductive walk as she strolled through the bullpen. Everyone took notice.

Laz willed her to look in his direction. *Just one look.*

As if sensing his gaze on her, she turned her head slightly and their eyes met. Air lodged in his throat and his pulse did a giddy-up as he took in her dark almond-shaped eyes that enhanced her smooth, lovely face. After her gaze lingered, she gave a slight nod at him before diverting her attention.

Despite her being clear across the bullpen, they were so attuned. Every nerve in his body came alive whenever she was around and it was as if he could feel her. He couldn't explain it better than that. The experience was baffling and fascinating at the same time.

"Lazarus! Get in here!" his sergeant yelled again, ruining the moment.

"Yeah, yeah. I'm coming," he mumbled, his attention still on Journey as he glimpsed her perfectly round ass and those long legs that he'd dreamed about having wrapped around his waist. He was a leg man and hers stood out beneath her fitted skirt, tapering down to a pair of tall, sexy-as-sin shoes.

Today her footwear was royal blue with a thin strap around the ankle, pulling out the royal blue accent color on her flawless tailored black suit. He had never been so fascinated by a woman's footwear and how they made her legs look until Journey came along.

Always dressed to the nines, she commanded attention not only in the courtroom when prosecuting a case, but also at his precinct. She never failed to have every man in the building, married or not, taking a second look.

"So have you seen the ADA's shoe collection up close

and personal yet?" Ashton whispered, now standing next to Laz. "Seeing that I haven't seen her wear the same pair twice, I'd say she has quite the collection. At least a hundred pairs."

Laz pulled his gaze away from the ADA and gave his head a slight shake, as if that would loosen the fog the sight of Journey always caused. What the hell was it about that woman? For the past few years, just the sight of her did something to him.

He wouldn't call them friends, exactly. They had more like a working relationship. A history. Though most encounters with each other resulted in arguments regarding her accusing him of jeopardizing her cases, there was still a mutual sexual tension that sparked between them. He never pursued her, but he'd often thought about it.

"Well?" Ashton prompted.

Laz frowned. "Well, what?"

Ashton looked at him as if he was crazy. "Uh, the shoe collection. Have you seen it?"

"Like I'd ever tell." Laz weaved around desks and chairs, heading to his boss's office. He knew Ashton's question had more to do with whether or not he and Journey had gotten naked yet, more than it had to do with her shoe collection. If anything juicy ever transpired between Journey and him, that would be one secret he'd keep close to his chest.

"You wanted to see me, Sarg?"

Sgt. Duane Ford tossed his pen onto his desk and leaned back in his office chair that squeaked, protesting his weight. "Close the door."

Laz did as instructed and turned his attention to his boss. Ford folded his arms across his chest. If he knew how much the move brought attention to his protruding beer belly, he'd probably stay hidden behind his desk.

"You want to tell me what happened to Scott Buckner's face? It looks like he slammed into a wall, several times."

Laz shrugged. "Hey, ask him."

"I did."

"And what did he say?"

"He said he fell. But I have a feeling there's more to it than that. Have a seat."

Laz dropped into the rickety wood chair in front of Ford and braced himself for the tongue-lashing he knew was coming.

Chapter Two

Frustration drummed through Journey Ramsey as she stuffed her tablet into her oversized handbag. She'd been in the interrogation room for the last twenty minutes, prepared to offer a deal to a suspect, but hadn't been able to take her mind off of Detective Lazarus Dimas. The man was a thorn in her side on most days, but damned if he didn't make her body quiver whenever he looked at her.

"Sorry about having you make a wasted trip down here, counselor," Detective Jones said when they left the interrogation room. He pulled the door closed, leaving his suspect cuffed to the metal table. "I thought having you present, with the promise of a deal, would get him to talk."

Journey shrugged. "You tried." They discussed next steps with the case. Again, Journey tried giving him her full attention, but knowing Laz could still be nearby had her anxious to get out of there. Not because she didn't want to see him. On the contrary. She loved looking at him, everything from his wind-tousled hair to those hazel-green eyes that seemed to look right through her.

No, she was ready to leave because if she happened to run into him, she might end up telling him something she had no business telling him. Something he needed to know, but coming from her could jeopardize her job, law license, and compromise the DA's office.

She said her goodbyes to the detective and moved through the bullpen where a nest of desks and cops were on the telephone or pecking away on their computers. It took all her willpower not to look in the direction of Laz's desk. She didn't want to give anyone a reason to think she was interested in him even though she was seriously attracted to him.

Who wouldn't be? The man was not only *fine*, but he had that intense, bad-boy vibe rolling off him in waves. The disheveled hair, muscular body, and that self-assured walk did something to her.

A door slammed to her left and she slowed. She couldn't stop her gaze from going in that direction even if she wanted to and...

Her breath hitched at the sight of Laz storming away from his boss's office. From the strong set of his jaw and the way he ran his hand through his dark hair, he wasn't happy. But God, was he beautiful to look at.

Laz glanced up and his piercing gaze locked on hers, diverting Journey's plan to keep walking toward the elevator.

Damn those eyes.

They bore into her like a heat-seeking missile charging toward its target. With the intensity behind his stare, it was a wonder she didn't trip over her feet. His gaze always seemed to take in everything around him, while also making her feel as if all of his attention was solely on her.

"Heading out?" he asked, his baritone voice like a whisper against her heated skin. He held the door open and then followed her out.

"Thanks," she mumbled trying to ignore the way his long-sleeved T-shirt stretched across his wide chest and hugged his thick arms. Even fully dressed, she could tell he was all muscle without a lick of fat anywhere.

Warmth spread through her body as he fell in step and walked down the hall with her as if they'd planned to leave together. Normally when they talked, or argued about a case mostly, it was out of earshot of others. Right now, she wasn't sure why he had followed her out.

As far as she was concerned, they had nothing to discuss, especially since in the last few minutes, she had made up her mind that she wouldn't share the information she'd learned less than seventy-two hours ago.

"Hey Laz, got a minute?"

Journey and Laz turned simultaneously toward the deep voice coming from where a police officer stood in the doorway of an office.

Laz turned back to her and moved in close. "Don't leave yet, all right? I want to talk to you," he said, his tone serious, his gaze unwavering.

Journey swallowed hard and watched as his easy gait carried him away without giving her a chance to respond.

Has he already heard about the investigation? No way. He wouldn't be this calm. Then again, maybe he's heard and wants to question me.

Journey shook the thought free. There was no way he knew.

She stepped out of the middle of the hallway, toward the elevator, debating on whether to leave or to wait for Laz. If by chance he'd heard what was going on, she didn't want him asking her any questions, especially since she couldn't tell him anything.

But Laz had a way about him. A way that made her want to succumb to his will. She hated the out-of-control feeling that seized her lately when it came to him.

"Well, well, well. If it isn't the DA's golden child."

Journey rolled her eyes, not bothering to turn around and acknowledge her coworker, attorney Gabriel Hall. For the most part, she liked the people she worked with, but Gabe could fall off the face of the earth and she'd be the last person to go looking for him.

"Funny running into you," he said, now standing alongside her. "Are you here to have lunch with your thug cop? Oops, I mean thug detective. You know, it's a shame you couldn't find a brotha to knock boots with, especially in a city loaded with them."

Journey turned and glared at him. She didn't have to ask who he was talking about, but was a little surprised he brought race into the one-sided conversation. A first. For some reason, Gabe had it in his head that she and Laz were sleeping together. He had walked in on them once in her office when they were having a heated conversation, and the bonehead took it as a lover's spat. He'd been giving her a hard time ever since.

What was it with this guy? Considering his childish behavior on occasion and some of the nonsense that usually fell from his mouth, she'd often wondered if his wealthy parents had purchased his law degree. Then again, probably not since she'd heard they'd kicked him out of the family for some stunt he'd pulled during college.

"So what? Nothing to say?" The stupid grin spread across his lips grated on her nerves.

"What the heck is your problem, Gabe? You clearly have an issue with me since every word out of your mouth lately has been meant to get under my skin. Why is that? Is it because I'm not interested in you?"

His hand went to his chest and he made a gagging sound as if the thought was ludicrous.

Journey looked him up and down, exhibiting as much disdain as possible. He was a good-looking man, with honey-brown skin and a nice build, but his funky attitude would be a total turn off had she been interested.

"Or is it that you're jealous of me? Do you feel threatened because I'm a better attorney than you are? Or does your poor attitude have anything to do with the fact that I'm the new ADA while you're barely able to maintain the title of prosecutor?"

She had recently been awarded the position, and though she was honored to get the promotion, it gave her even more pleasure knowing she had beat out Gabe for the job. He had looked down on her from the moment she stepped into the

DA's office eight years ago. Knowing that he would give his firstborn for the title, it pleased her to taunt him whenever he gave her a hard time.

His features twisted into an evil scowl and he got in her face. "My merits alone made me the better choice, but I guess if you kiss the boss's a—"

"Go to hell. You would've been the last person the DA chose." Now she was angry, her scowl as deep as his. "From what I've seen, you've had your paralegals doing all of your work. Either one of them would deserve the next ADA job before you."

"You win a few big cases lately and suddenly you're walking around acting as if you're queen of the office. You ain't shit, Journey," he spat. "The sooner you realize that, the better off we'll all be. The only reason you've gotten as far as you have is because the powers that be want to tap that ass."

Journey's jaw dropped open and disbelief engulfed her. There was no love between them, but even when their comments were snarky, they'd always kept their interactions professional. The hatred glowing in his eyes and the disdain in his tone now caught her off guard.

"Everything all right over here?"

Journey swung around to find Laz standing behind them. She hadn't heard him approach, but by the malevolent glare he bore into Gabe, he'd overheard some of their conversation.

"Just peachy, officer," Gabe snarled and stomped away.

Journey's heart pounded rapidly as her gaze followed Gabe down the hall. It was no secret they didn't like each other, but his words stung and had her wondering if something else was going on.

Why would he say something like that if he hadn't heard it somewhere? Were the men in the office discussing her? Did they feel the same way as Gabe regarding her being awarded the ADA position?

"You all right?" Laz asked, concern in his eyes as he pushed the down button for the elevator.

Oh great. She'd been standing in front of the elevator and hadn't even pushed the button. "I'm fine," she snapped a little harsher than intended, still trying to shake off Gabe's words.

It was as if Laz knew she needed a moment to gather herself. Silence fell between them as they waited for the elevator.

"You want to tell me what that was all about?"

"Not really."

Again, silence. Seconds ticked by for a moment Journey thought he'd drop the subject, but then he spoke

"If the jerk is giving you trouble, tell me. I'll handle him 'cause I really don't like the shithead."

Journey couldn't stop the smile from spreading across her face, nor the laugh that bubbled inside her throat. "Yeah, me neither."

"Do you still work with that nonprofit agency, Save Our Boys?" he asked, thankfully jumping to a different subject.

Save Our Boys was an organization she'd been first introduced to by Tony, her ex-boyfriend, who had once benefitted from the program and currently sat on the board of directors. The agency focused on young men from age fourteen to twenty-five who endured some type of violence and abuse or needed guidance in life. It also supported those whose family had been ripped apart by drugs and addiction. Getting the boys off the streets and into programs like apprenticeships, career training, and anything else that gave the kids a shot at having a successful life was a big part of their mission.

"Yeah, why?" she finally asked.

"There's this kid, Scott, who I had an, um…run-in with today. I think he could benefit from their services. Do you have any contact information with you?"

Journey narrowed her eyes at him, stuck on the word "run-in." When it came to Laz, that could mean anything and probably nothing good. Instead of questioning him, she dug into her oversized bag and tore a slip of paper from her small notebook. Scribbling a name and number on it, she handed the paper to him.

"This is their office number, but it might be better for you to take Scott there personally. Most kids don't go willingly."

He nodded and slid the paper into the front pocket of his jeans. "How's it going with the Turner case?" he asked.

Laz asking about the Turner case made her think of the other case she'd been debating on telling him about. The one that could possibly land him in jail.

"We had to let Turner walk."

"What?" he ground between gritted teeth and faced her full-on. "What the hell, Journey? That case was solid. There's no way he should've walked."

Laz only called her by her first name when no one else was within ear shot. Clearly he had no idea of the affect his presence had on her, the way her body hummed with lust when he stared at her the way he was doing now, otherwise he'd back the hell up. Or risk her grabbing the front of his shirt and pulling him in for a searing kiss.

How could she have a crush on a man—a cop—who pushed the boundaries of justice while alienating his superiors at every turn? The city streets were safer because he was on the force, but he walked a thin line between following the law and being a criminal himself. They might've been on the same side of the law, but he went against everything she stood for. She couldn't condone someone who took justice into his own hands at every turn, often jeopardizing her cases by not following procedure.

Journey hated being attracted to him. Hated that she longed to be wrapped in his muscular arms. And she hated that she'd give almost anything to taste his lips just once. And more than anything, she wished there was a way to ignore whatever this was between them.

She didn't speak until they stepped onto the elevator, and when she did, she kept her voice low knowing there were cameras. "There wasn't enough evidence to hold Turner."

"Bullshit! That was a clean arrest and you know it. Besides that, two witnesses put him at the scene and his prints were on the weapon."

"So were a ton of other prints from people at that party. And as for the witnesses, they recanted and Turner had an alibi; a weak one, but one nonetheless."

Laz slapped his palm against the back wall of the elevator. He didn't speak, but she could almost hear the gears in his head turning, trying to figure out what he'd need to do to get Turner behind bars.

Turner was a known drug dealer with ties to organized crime. Law enforcement had been trying to nail him for over a year. Laz was the best detective on the force, and relentless when digging for answers. No doubt Turner would eventually screw up and Laz would be there to capitalize on his mistake and finally get this guy once and for all.

Laz's passion to get criminals off the street was admirable, but Journey had often wondered what drove him. It wasn't until recently she'd found out about his girlfriend who had died during his first year as a detective. The details were sketchy, but Journey suspected that the girlfriend's death fueled the demons pushing Laz.

Journey studied his profile, taking note of the wisp of gray hair near his temple. He was in his late thirties, early forties, with thick dark hair that curled slightly at his collar. Gone was the short ponytail he used to sport. During a conversation years ago, he'd mentioned his parents were deceased; his father of Greek descent and his mother, Irish. No doubt he was a perfect blending of the best of his parents' features. The man was exquisite.

Still leaning against the back wall, Laz turned and searched her eyes. "What else?"

Her brows dipped. "Excuse me?"

"What else, Journey? There's something else on your mind, and I'm not talking about whatever issue is going on with that chump, Hall. When you stepped into the bullpen earlier and you saw me, I could see it in your eyes.

Something's bothering you."

All she could do was stare at him. Could he read minds? Debating on whether to give him a heads-up or not weighed heavy on her mind. She owed him. Laz had saved her life a couple of years ago after she'd been attacked by a man on her way to the MARTA station to catch the train home.

She shuddered as the scene of blood and ripped clothing flashed in her mind, reminding her of how terrified she'd been. But then Laz had come out of nowhere, tackling the man, beating him to within an inch of his life. To this day, she didn't even want to think about what would've happened to her if he hadn't shown up. She would forever be indebted to him.

Journey quickly diverted her gaze from his even though she knew he couldn't read minds. He was playing her. Trying to extract information out of her the way he masterfully did with so many of his collars.

No. This was something she had to keep to herself right now. She'd figure out another way to help him.

She released a long breath as the elevator doors opened. "There's nothing else," she finally said, "but if you find anything on Turner, make sure it's something my office can use."

Laz followed her out of the elevator. "What difference would it make? The guy probably skipped town the moment the cuffs were off." Laz continued walking with her. When they stepped outside he touched her arm, forcing her to stop. "Why do I feel there's something else on your mind?"

"Of course there are other things on my mind, Laz. I have a ton of open cases. I'm tired and I haven't had a day off in six months."

He gazed into her eyes as if searching for a clue. She was a lawyer who rarely backed down, but damn if he didn't have her squirming inside. It was as if he could see right through her.

She glanced at her watch, anything to break eye contact with this man who set her body on fire with just a look. What was it about him that made her want to leap into his arms and grind her body against his?

She shivered at the thought, knowing it was a fantasy that would never come to fruition.

"Detective, I'd love to stand here while you try to read me, but I have to be in court shortly. Besides, I'm sure you have more bad guys to get off the street."

He nodded, but still didn't look convinced. "All right. I'll let you go, but I'll be in touch…soon."

Laz strutted back into the building without another word and without a glance back.

Why did his words feel more like a promise than just a figure of speech?

"And why did he have to make them sound so darn sexy?" Journey blew out an unsteady breath and shook herself before walking away. "He is off-limits. He is definitely off-limits," she mumbled to herself.

Now, if only her words could make her body cooperate.

Chapter Three

Hours later, Laz sat at his desk and twirled a pen between his fingers. The heated discussion between Journey and Gabriel Hall bothered him. He'd only caught the tail end of the argument, but he had heard enough to make him want to snatch up Hall and slam his ass against the wall for the things he'd said to her.

What bugged him more was the conversation he'd had with Journey. Something was bothering her and he had a nagging feeling it had nothing to do with Hall, but everything to do with him. An intense sexual vibe had always existed between them, but today's energy had nothing to do with his attraction to her.

Today was different. Journey had been different. There was something she wasn't telling him.

Laz glanced up from his desk and watched two guys in suits head to Sergeant Ford's office. He recognized one of them as an internal affairs investigator. Hell, he should know all of them by now considering the number of times he'd been investigated, especially lately.

Knowing they were there for him, Laz grabbed his keys from the top of the desk and eased toward the back door. He would answer their fifty million questions, but not today.

"Not so fast." Sergeant Ford's deep baritone stopped

Laz in his tracks.

He cursed under his breath and turned slowly to find one of the suits standing next to Ford, a smug look on the man's face.

"Let's talk, detective. Shall we?" With a dramatic wave of his arm, the guy pointed toward the conference room.

"Might as well. Let's just get this over with."

*

Laz slouched in the uncomfortable chair he'd been sitting in for the past hour, nearing the end of his patience. He usually got a thrill out of pissing the higher-ups off, especially if he ended up with the last laugh by proving that he'd made a clean bust. However, these internal affairs investigations were getting old, and a little too frequent for his liking.

With his union rep sitting next to him, Laz answered one question after another, some more than once, regarding the investigation into a shooting he'd been involved in recently. Henry Gaines, the IA investigator, was relentless, but knowing he had done everything right in the incident, Laz tolerated the questioning. At least for a while.

When he first followed Gaines into the conference room, he thought the interrogation would center around Scott's arrest. Granted, that would've been a quick turnaround, but if history was any indication, when it came to trying to pin something on him, IA didn't waste time. Laz could admit to crossing a multitude of lines in regards to Scott. His sergeant had even threatened to suspend him…again. But if in the long run Laz's actions got Scott on the straight and narrow, it would be worth any fallout.

"So, let's go over the details again, Detective Dimas," Gaines said, interrupting Laz's musings. "Walk me through what happened as you were leaving the restaurant?"

Fury stabbed Laz in the chest. "What the hell, man? I've told you the same shit two times already!"

"Detective," the union rep ground out in a warning tone as he narrowed his eyes.

Laz gritted his teeth, tapping down his anger before surrendering to giving the details yet again.

"Before my shift started that day, I stopped to pick up lunch. While I was paying for my order at the deli, I glanced out the window and noticed a couple of guys arguing on the sidewalk."

"And then what happened?" Gaines asked as if he wasn't hearing the story for the third time.

"When I walked outside, the perp—Corwin—was talking smack to the other guy. I thought maybe it was just a little disagreement, so I hung back until I heard Corwin say, 'you're about to find out what happens when you steal from me.'

"It wasn't until he pulled a gun from his back waistband that I dropped my bag of food and pulled out my weapon. I identified myself as a police officer and Corwin whirled around. At first he had the gun trained on the man he was arguing with, then he turned it on me."

"Go on."

Irritation crawled through Laz at the condescending way the IA investigator said *go on*, as if he was dealing with some Joe-blow witness off the street.

Laz leaned forward, his forearms on the conference room table more than ready to be done with the questioning. "I told him to drop his weapon. Instead, he fired at me. Had the guy been a better shot, I'd be dead right now. Oh wait, you probably don't give a damn about that though, huh?"

"Detective, I don't need the commentary, just the details of what transpired."

Laz sat back in his chair, rubbed his forehead and sighed. "After the punk shot at me, he took off and I gave chase, warning him to stop. He knocked over a few people on the street and I yelled for everyone to get down. Corwin stopped, turned and pointed his gun at me again. I shot him twice and he dropped to the ground."

Gaines sighed and tapped his pen against his notepad, eyeing Laz as if he didn't believe him.

"So you're saying that at this point in the incident, the guy ran and *then* stopped, turned and shot at you again?"

Laz bolted out of his seat. "I've repeated the exact same story three times in the last hour. I'm not sure what type of bullshit you're trying to drum up, but I'm done." He headed to the door and didn't stop until the union rep lunged from his seat and called out to him.

Laz glanced over his shoulder, his hand on the door knob.

The IA guy hadn't moved, but said, "Detective, it's my job to provide accountability to the department. So I have to ask these questions and get a good understanding of what happened. You're not doing yourself any favors by not cooperating."

"Not cooperating!" Laz balled his hands into a fist at his side, unable to control the anger scorching every nerve ending in his body. "What do you think I've been doing for the past hour? Why do I have to keep repeating myself?"

"Because a couple of witnesses have different stories."

"I don't give a damn what a witness said! I've been on this force for over seventeen years working my *ass* off. All of a sudden, my word isn't good enough?"

"I'm not saying that. I just want to make sure we have all the facts and the whole story."

"I gave you the whole story over and over again. To hell with this investigation. If you want to arrest me, arrest me. If you want to suspend me, fine. If you want to fire my ass, have at it. But don't fuck with my intelligence. I've given my life to this department and for what? This bullshit?" Laz slammed the side of his fist against the door. "You guys have been trying to nail me for one incident or another for years now."

Gaines pounded on the table, causing water from his paper cup to spill over the rim. "That's because you keep giving us reason to!"

Laz had been able to easily defend himself in the last five IA investigations, but he was becoming sick of even trying now. All of the questioning, the harassing, wasn't worth it. He knew the law and department procedure, but sometimes, to get the job done, he had to skate on the edge of both.

With other cases, he understood why they investigated, but even during those instances they only heard what they wanted to. Like the case where a perp complained that Laz had been too rough when patting him down. The guy hadn't mentioned that he'd swung at Laz and resisted arrest while being checked for weapons.

In another case, there'd been a complaint that he used harsh language, had a bad attitude and wouldn't listen to the offender. It didn't matter that the guy was crawling out of a window after sexually assaulting a woman.

In this case, he had done everything right and still he was being questioned. He knew it had to do more with the offender being black and Laz being white. IA's hands were tied since the community was in an uproar, but Laz refused to be harassed because of doing his job.

"Gaines, whether you believe me or not, I did everything by the book. Mind you, I was off duty. Would you have preferred me to walk away and let the situation escalate without doing anything?"

The investigator said nothing.

"No, I'm sure you wouldn't have wanted me to do that because if I had and it got back to you guys, then I'd be under a whole different investigation. I've vowed to serve this city whether on duty or off and that's exactly what I did."

"Dimas...I'm just trying to do my job."

"And that's exactly what I was doing. You know as well as anyone, when we're out on those streets, we have to often make split-second decisions. That perp knew I was a cop, yet he ignored my instructions *and* fired at me. What would you have wanted me to do in that situation?"

"I wasn't there so I—"

"But I was there and I told you everything that happened. I shouldn't have to keep repeating myself."

"The detective is right." The union rep finally spoke up.

"He's answered all of your questions and…"

Laz tuned out the rest as he inhaled and exhaled a few times to get his anger under control. He was tempted to say *to hell with it all* and turn in his weapon and badge.

But he couldn't. At least not yet. There were still too many youths getting caught up in the system, and drug dealers evading the law. He had vowed that as long as he was on the force, he'd make a difference. He'd do his part in making the streets safe for kids, and more importantly, get as many drugs off the streets as possible.

But accomplishing either objective was starting to look bleak and unattainable.

And honestly, Laz didn't know how much more he could take.

Chapter Four

Journey awkwardly shifted her laptop bag and a vase of roses in her arms as she pushed open the door to her condo.

Maybe I should've accepted the doorman's assistance when he offered to help carry some of this stuff.

Feeling the glass vase slipping from her grasp, she quickly set it on the tall table near the entrance and sighed with relief.

"Home sweet home," she mumbled, flipping on the lights as she lowered her bag to the floor and then leaned against the door. "These long days have to stop."

Undoing the ankle buckle on her shoes, Journey kicked off the footwear, not caring that they landed in the middle of the floor. After the twelve-hour-day she had just put in, all she wanted to do was have a glass of wine, find something to eat, and then take a nice, long bubble bath.

In the living room, she shrugged out of her suit jacket, dropping it on the sofa as she strolled to the windows, relishing the feel of the plush carpet beneath her feet.

"This is worth every ridiculous penny," she said of the spectacular view outside. The stress of the day slowly slipped from her body as she released a long satisfying breath.

She stared out into the night, admiring the twinkling lights of nearby buildings overlooking the Buckhead area. Her view from the twenty-fifth floor was breathtaking, no matter the time of day, and whenever she was at home, she found herself standing in front of the window looking out. Moving in eight months ago, shortly after breaking up with her long-time boyfriend, Tony, Journey had fulfilled her goal of living in a high-rise.

She admitted she missed her ex, especially after being together two years. But their break-up was inevitable. He wanted marriage. She didn't.

Journey startled when the intercom buzzed and glanced at her watch. It was after nine. Normally the doorman didn't ring her up this time of night unless she had a visitor or food being delivered. She wasn't expecting either.

She pushed the button on the wall near the door. "Yes."

"Ms. Ramsey, sorry to bother you, ma'am, but there is a Detective Dimas here to see you."

Journey froze, her finger hovering over the speak button. *What the heck is he doing here?*

"Ms. Ramsey?" the doorman called out after a few seconds.

"I'm sorry, Frankie. Please send him up."

Journey glanced around. She quickly nudged her heels out of the middle of the floor, not caring that the pile of shoes in the foyer was starting to build. As she peered into the living room, she gasped at the clothing strewn on a chair, on the back of the sofa, and her chaise lounge. The cleaning lady came once a week and she certainly wasn't magically appearing in the next thirty seconds to straighten up.

She quickly snatched three blazers from the chair, a skirt, blouse, and jacket from the sofa. With her arms full, she glanced around frantically looking for a place to stash them, but a knock sounded at the door.

Too late.

After a moment of hesitation, Journey blew out a breath and dropped the items back in the chair. She headed to the door but stopped at the mirror in the foyer to check her hair. She ran her fingers through her short, permed strands before trying to smooth the wrinkles from the tail of her blouse.

She stopped abruptly. *Why the heck am I doing this? Just because he stopped by unannounced doesn't mean I should try to make everything perfect.*

Journey yanked open the door, prepared to give him a piece of her mind for just dropping by, but that didn't happen. Like usual, the sight of Laz screwed with her equilibrium. Her heart thumped wildly inside of her chest as he stood nonchalantly, all brawn and virile, against the door jamb.

Why'd he have to be so gorgeous?

"I was wondering if you were ever going to answer the door." Laz remained where he was as if he didn't have a care in the world, his striking eyes sparkling with mischief.

Swallowing hard, it took Journey a moment to form a coherent thought. "What are you doing here?"

He pulled a small white bag from behind his back and the smell of meat, onions, and peppers delighted her senses. "Thought you might be hungry. Besides, I told you I'd catch you later," he said in a just-woke-up-from-a-deep-sleep rasp. The sensuous tone reminded her of the night he'd come to her rescue. After calling in the crime, he had held her close, and the comforting words he whispered in her ear were soothing and calmed her until the EMTs arrived.

Journey opened the door wider and he entered. The fresh and clean scent of his cologne drifting past her nostrils almost made her moan.

God, he smelled good.

"I assumed when you said you would see me later that it was just an expression. A figure of speech. How'd you even know where I lived?"

She gave herself a mental slap the moment the words left her mouth. She rolled her eyes at the way his raised brows mocked her. There wasn't much this man didn't know or couldn't find out.

He strolled into the living room, looking around as if casing the joint. She was proud of her condo. Despite it not being overly neat, it was expertly decorated, comfortable and had killer views. She watched him stop in front of the windows.

"How long have you lived here?"

"What, you don't know? You seem to know everything else."

He glanced over his shoulder. "I could find out, but maybe I want to learn some things directly from you."

She stared, dumbfounded, unsure of what to say. Instead of responding, she walked the few steps into the kitchen.

"Though I didn't invite you here, I guess I could at least offer you something to drink."

One of the things that attracted her to the fourteen-hundred square foot condominium was the open floor plan. She could stand in one spot and see everything except for the two bedrooms and two bathrooms. "I have water, juice, and wine."

She looked back to find him eyeing her. One of her pet peeves was people who stopped by her place without calling first. Though she should be irritated, she had to admit it was kind of nice seeing him outside of work. Standing at over six feet tall and two-hundred-plus pounds, with wide shoulders, and jeans just tight enough to show off thick thighs, she could look at him all day.

"I didn't realize you were such a slob," he cracked, snapping Journey out of her trance.

"You know what? You can leave." She pointed her thumb toward the door, trying not to laugh even when he chuckled.

"Hey, don't get mad at me because I speak the truth." He sobered. "Who are the flowers from?"

She glanced toward the entrance though she couldn't actually see the flowers from where she stood. Neither could he, which amazed her. He'd only been in the foyer for a hot second, yet he'd probably noticed every single element in the space.

"How do you know I didn't buy them?"

He chuckled again and moved away from the window. His gaze swept the open space, taking in the white, plush furniture and carpet before directing his attention back to her.

"One, they're sitting by the door, haphazardly on the edge of the table. If you had bought them, they'd probably be in the center of that fancy dining room table, on the breakfast bar, or maybe on the sofa table."

"Two," he moved to the center of the living room, "this whole area is stark white except for a little black on the backsplash in the kitchen. The roses jump out like blood splatter on white concrete. They don't fit in."

Journey just stared, fascinated by the way his brain worked. Sometimes in talking with him, it seemed as if everything was like a clue to him, and he didn't rest until each piece of evidence was in place.

This was the first time she'd had a man, besides her father, in her new space and at the moment, she couldn't think of anyone else she'd rather have there.

The thought unnerved her, yet there was a little spark of excitement jockeying around inside her gut, but she pushed the feeling down. Laz had a reputation. Though she thought—no, she *knew*—he was a good guy, there were rumors that he was a rogue cop. Those in law enforcement either liked or hated him. Very few people were in between. In her opinion, he was a good detective whose intentions were honorable even if they weren't always legal.

"And three," Laz continued, now standing within reach of her.

Starting from the top of her head, his eyes drank her in inch by inch and didn't stop until he reached her bare feet. All she could do was stand there and let him get his fill, her body heating everywhere his gaze landed. This man was a detriment to her willpower and her brain function. Because with the way he was looking at her, and the lust racing through her body, all he had to do was say the word and she'd drop her panties in a heartbeat.

How crazy was that?

"You don't strike me as a rose type of person. You're more of a tulip or orchid type of woman." He moved even closer. "You're soft, delicate, yet sophisticated, and damned if you don't smell sweet."

Journey gulped. "How do you know I'm soft? You've never touched me," she said quietly. The words were out of her mouth before she could stop them.

"Not because I haven't wanted to." He brushed the back of his fingers down her cheek and her eyes drifted close as she leaned into his touch. When she reopened her eyes, seconds ticked by as they stared at each other, his gaze lingering on her mouth.

Laz cursed and mumbled something under his breath just before he lowered his head and brushed his lips across hers, making her mouth tingle.

Journey's brain screamed for her to stop him right there, not to go any further, but her body ached for him. No way was she pushing this intriguing man away. She'd fantasized about them coming together more times than she could count.

No. She wanted this. She wanted *him.*

His kiss was gentle and unhurried as his tongue explored the interior of her mouth, sending currents of desire lapping at every nerve in her body. She moaned when his strong arm went around her waist and he pulled her against his hard powerful body. Her nipples beaded at the contact as the throb between her thighs increased. Not only was he the sexiest specimen she'd ever seen but he could kiss, too.

"God, Journey," Laz groaned against her mouth and dropped his arm from around her waist as he lifted his head slightly. He didn't seem to want to stop any more than she did. His eyes met hers as if asking permission to go further. She said nothing. Instead she placed her hand on his chest, fisting his T-shirt, and pulled him back against her body.

That little sampling wasn't nearly enough.

*

Laz cupped her face between his hands, succumbing to

the gravitational pull that had been between them since the first time they'd met. He knew he should stop and back the hell away before he lost total control, but he had waited too long for this moment. He had waited too long to be this close to her without getting just a little taste. No way was he stopping.

God, she felt good and soft rubbed up against him. His hands slid down the sides of her body and lowered to her firm butt as he drank in the sweetness of her lips. He deepened the kiss, holding her closer knowing she could feel how hard she made him.

Journey moaned as his tongue danced with hers, familiarizing itself with every nook and cranny of her luscious mouth. All the desire he'd had pent up over the years to kiss her came to the forefront as he savored every moment. This connection exceeded his expectations and when her hands slid into his hair, he just about lost it. His body throbbed with need. But just as quick as the kiss started, common sense settled over him like a cold chill.

They couldn't do this.

He was no good for her.

If she ever got involved with him, his reputation alone would ruin her good name. Laz couldn't let that happen.

Knowing this, he reluctantly broke off the kiss, but was slow to release her. They were like two magnets molded together and it was almost impossible to pull away. He needed to…he should…but he couldn't, at least not yet.

Journey took her time opening her alluring eyes and he easily got lost in the dreaminess of them. This woman had a hold on him that he couldn't explain. And now that he'd kissed her, he was screwed. If she had any idea how much power she had over him, she could do some serious damage to his heart. Good thing she'd never know.

Laz dropped his hands and Journey visibly shivered before clearing her throat.

"Um, how about that drink?" She hurried away from him, pouring herself a glass of wine, and taking a huge gulp.

Laz released a noisy breath and ran his hands through his hair, glad to know he wasn't the only one affected by their intense lip-lock. Making himself at home, he reached into the refrigerator, not surprised that there was very little food since she spent most of her days at the office. Yet, she had plenty to drink. He grabbed a bottle of water and moved to the other side of the long counter, where she'd set the burritos he'd brought.

He pointed at their food. "Let's eat. I'm starving."

He waited until she was seated at the breakfast bar before snagging the stool next to her. They ate in silence, each lost in their own thoughts. What he needed to do was find out what she'd been holding back from him earlier, but first he had to get his body under control. Only minutes ago, flames of desire consumed him like the hottest fire, singeing every cell within him. He hadn't felt this worked up in a while. Sure, he'd been with plenty of women over the years, but not one had him ready to say to hell with everything in order to have her. He hadn't felt like this since...not since Gwenn.

Don't go there, Dimas. He definitely didn't need to travel down that mental road.

"The flowers were from a client," Journey said out of nowhere.

Laz nodded, not bothering to ask if the client was male or female. It was best he didn't know.

"Are you ready to tell me what you wanted to say earlier?" he finally asked Journey, tossing the wrapper from his burrito into the trash. He poured more wine into her glass before grabbing another bottle of water for himself. "Talk to me. What's going on?"

She wrapped her hands around her wineglass and he could feel the tension bouncing off her.

"What's wrong? Are you in trouble? Is it a case? Because whatever it is, I know it's bothering you." He touched her hand and she looked at him. "You can trust me. Tell me what happened."

"Laz, I could lose my job—or worse, be disbarred if I say anything right now."

Okay, so this is serious.

"Is there something I can do to help?" he asked quietly. If she was in trouble, there wasn't anything he wouldn't do. He couldn't explain his possessiveness when it came to her. He wasn't even sure when his feelings for her had grown so strong.

"Be careful of the people around you," she whispered, staring at her wineglass.

He stiffened. The words were spoken so quietly, he almost didn't hear them.

"So this is about me?" he asked cautiously.

She gave a slight nod of her head before turning her troubled gaze in his direction. His heart squeezed. Not so much for himself, but for the worry he saw in her eyes.

"I can't tell you anything more yet, but for now, Laz, just…watch your back."

Chapter Five

"What do you mean he kissed you? And you're just now telling me?"

Journey pulled the cell phone away from her ear, smiling when her sister Geneva screamed. She was the only person in the world who knew about the crush Journey had on Laz. Now, based on the number of questions her sister was firing off, maybe she should've kept that bit of information to herself.

"Geneva, it's no big deal. It's just something that happened." Journey leaned her hip against the counter in her office's break room and ripped open a sugar packet, pouring it into her black coffee. She'd been at her desk for five hours straight and hadn't accomplished anything thanks to thinking about Laz. That's why she called her sister, hoping she could take her mind off of him.

Clearly that wasn't going to happen.

"Journey, this is a big deal. That kiss means your feelings for each other are mutual. Why the hell are you guys fighting this attraction?"

"We sorta work together and it would be weird on too many levels if we got together," Journey whispered into the phone, not knowing when someone would walk in. She didn't bother telling her sister that getting with Laz would also be a bad idea because of his reputation. She had worked too hard to get where she was today to let poor decisions taint her efforts. And Laz would definitely be a poor decision. At least that's what she kept telling herself.

He was bad for her, but boy, did she want him. The kiss they'd shared the other day had rocked her, making her want so much more. How many times had she fantasized about what it would be like to be with him, cradled in his strong arms as they made love? That sampling the other day, when he'd kissed her senseless, assured her they'd be great together.

She hadn't had sex in almost eight months, not since Tony, and her vibrator wasn't getting the job done. Laz would be the perfect candidate to scratch the itch her equipment couldn't reach. Would he think her too forward if she propositioned him? It could be a win-win situation since neither of them were the serious relationship type. At least she didn't think he was. Then again, she really didn't know all that much about him.

"Okay, sis. We're not done with this conversation, but I have to go. My client just showed up." As a hairstylist with a high-end clientele, Geneva stayed busy. Meaning with her own hectic schedule, they rarely saw each other.

"All right. I need to get going, too. I have to be in court in a couple of hours. I'll talk to you later."

"Don't talk to me, Journey. Talk to him! You know you want to." Her sister disconnected before Journey could respond. As usual, Geneva was right. Journey did want to talk to Laz, but she would much rather kiss him again.

Journey noted the time on the microwave that was sitting on the counter next to the sink. She still had almost two hours before she had to be in court, but needed to do a little work on another case before leaving. Still thinking about the conversation with her sister, she topped off her coffee, wondering if she should make a play for Laz. Letting a man know that she was interested was something her sister would do, but for Journey, that was way out of her comfort zone.

She shook her head in an effort to lose the thought.

What she needed to be focused on was work. Besides, if Laz did have anything to do with mishandling the Monsuli case, the last thing she should do was get involved with him.

So what if I can't stop thinking about him. He's off-limits.

Journey stepped out of the break room and almost ran into her paralegal, Casey.

"Oh, there you are. I was getting ready to put these in your office," she said, holding a beautiful flower arrangement. "They just arrived for you."

Journey frowned. "For me?" This was the second time in only a few days that she had received flowers. Before then, she couldn't remember the last time someone sent her anything.

"Yep, and I can't wait to find out who they're from."

Thinking the same thing, Journey accepted the crystal vase and really took notice of the arrangement. After a few moments, a smile threatened to break free. No way had *he* sent her a large bouquet of orchids. *He* being Laz.

Or had he? she thought turning the crystal vase slightly in search of a card as she and Casey headed to Journey's office. After hearing Laz explain why red roses didn't fit her, she couldn't help but wonder, and almost hoped the flowers were from him.

"Ooh, those are gorgeous."

"I wish someone would send me flowers."

Some of the office staff said as they passed them in the hallway. Journey knew the grin on her face was probably larger than it needed to be, but she couldn't help it. The orchids were exquisite and smelled divine.

"Is there a new boyfriend on the scene or is Tony trying to win you back?" Casey asked the moment they stepped into Journey's office. She leaned against the desk and rubbed her palms together, anxiously waiting to determine the identity of the mystery sender.

She and Casey had worked together for the last three years and hit it off from day one. In her mid-forties, with long strawberry-blonde hair, blue eyes, and a sunny disposition,

Casey was sharper than some lawyers. For years Journey had tried to get the woman to pursue a law degree, but Casey always waved her off claiming she preferred being in a support role.

"No new boyfriend, and Tony really wasn't the flower-sending type," Journey eventually said. Plucking the small envelope from the bouquet, she pulled out the note card.

Now these are more like you. Delicate. Soft. Sweet-smelling.

Journey laughed. The words weren't exactly poetic, but the thoughtful gesture let her know that Laz had the potential of being a romantic. Who knew? A big, bad guy like him clearly hiding his softer side.

"Hmm…" Casey said, narrowing her eyes. "They might not be from a boyfriend, but whoever they're from must be a potential boyfriend if that grin is any indication. And are you blushing?"

Smiling harder, Journey shook her head and moved items around on her desk to make room for the vase. "Have you ever seen a black person blush?"

"Can't say that I have, but if I'm not mistaken, I do see a reddish tint painting your cheeks."

"Okay, maybe I am blushing a little, but these are from…a friend." She couldn't really say that she and Laz were friends, but if she was honest with herself, she did consider him a friend. He was trustworthy, fun to be around, though a pain at times, and more importantly, he had come through for her when she needed him the most.

Casey pushed away from the desk and stood to her full height. "Do I know this…friend?"

Journey's shrug was noncommittal. "Maybe, but maybe not."

"Mmhm. I'm going to be watching you, Missy. I have a feeling you're not being on the up-and-up with me, but that's okay. Keep him a secret. You know I'm the research queen," she said as she headed to the door. "If I really want to know who this mystery man is, I have my ways." Journey laughed at the way Casey squinted and pointed at her.

"I know, I know, but there's nothing to research here. He's just a friend. If ever I get a boyfriend again, you'll be the first to know."

"Damn straight I will, but for now, I'll let it go since you need to prepare for court. Chop, chop."

She was right. There was just enough time to double-check that she had everything she needed.

But first...

Journey dialed Laz's number.

"Well, what do I owe the pleasure? Let me guess, you're calling to chew me out about another case," he said by way of greeting, his voice low and sexy.

"Though I'm sure you've probably screwed up yet another one," she joked, "I'm actually calling to thank you. You've made my day. The flowers are lovely."

"Glad you like them, and it's good to know I could make your day."

If only he knew.

Journey wasn't starving for a man's attention; actually, she didn't have time to be concerned about the opposite sex. However, she had to admit that it felt good, even if it was platonic, to have Laz's attention. With his good looks and swagger, she was sure he wasn't hurting for female companionship. If anything, women were probably throwing themselves at him.

"Well, that's all I called for. Thanks again for the flowers."

"My pleasure. What do you have planned for the rest of the day?" he asked.

"Actually, I need to be in court shortly, so I guess I should get off the phone and let you get back to whatever you were doing."

"All right, baby. Good luck in court. Give 'em hell."

"Thanks," she said, smiling and disconnected the call.

Journey held the phone to her chest, feeling a little giddy. How silly was it that him calling her *baby* could illicit a warm and tingling feeling inside of her? That short conversation reminded her of how much she missed having someone pulling for her, someone outside of her sister or parents. A man. A strong, virile, sexy man who made her hot and bothered with little effort.

Cool it, girl. Don't forget he might be involved in planting evidence.

Journey sighed and set her phone on the desk. She liked Laz, a lot, but jonesing after him was a bad idea. A very bad idea.

She'd do good to remember that.

Chapter Six

Hours later, Journey grinned as she stuffed files into her briefcase, unable to keep the elation she felt deep down inside from showing on her face. The day just kept getting better. She had just won a murder case for the state that she'd been working on for over a year. One of the most challenging cases of her career and she couldn't stop smiling.

After accepting several congratulatory praises from people filing out of the court room, she headed for the exit.

"Nice job, counselor," someone said to her left. She glanced over at the row of wooden benches and her smile grew.

"Why thank you, David." She and US Attorney David Lassiter had attended law school together. While she worked at the state level, David worked at the federal level and was one of the best lawyers she knew. "I didn't see you sitting over there. What brings you here?" she asked after they exchanged a hug.

"I had some business in the area and heard about your case, figured I'd stop in and see you in action."

They talked for a few minutes, reminiscing about old times and friends they hadn't seen in a while. After promising to meet for lunch one day soon, they went their separate ways. Since it was almost five o'clock, there were only a few people milling around the courthouse.

Journey shook out of her suit jacket and draped it through the handles of her briefcase as she strolled through the hallway past another courtroom, feeling as if she'd won a million bucks. She'd won her share of cases, but this one was special. Even now her heart ached for the homeless teenager who had died of a drug overdose. Whether the kid was a regular user or not, he was still a victim. If she had her way, every drug dealer alive would be behind bars or six feet under, and she was glad she wasn't the only one who felt that way.

The detectives on the case had been relentless. They had followed the trail to two small-time drug dealers and had arrested them months after the kid's death. It had been a long shot, but her office had been able to successfully prosecute the two men for murder.

Reflecting on the case, she couldn't help but think about Laz, who was one of the arresting detectives. His strong testimony weeks ago, as well as his partner's, had definitely helped the trial. Laz had tracked the two criminals like a man possessed, claiming there was no way they could let them walk after a young man had lost his life so senselessly. Journey knew his passion for justice in this case had more to do with his past loss.

"So, you won another case. I guess you're feeling proud of yourself."

And there went her good mood.

Journey kept walking, hoping her nemesis would disappear into a big black hole, but Gabe fell in step with her. She stopped and moved off to the side of the hallway.

"What do you want? Because I'm sure you're not here to congratulate me on my win." She adjusted the shoulder strap and moved her bulky bag in front of her. Gabe was a little too close, but she refused to back away. With his height and build, he might've been able to intimidate some of the people in the office and witnesses on the stand, but he didn't scare her.

They had crossed paths in the office, but hadn't had words since their encounter at the police station over a week ago, and she'd planned to keep it that way.

"Yeah, congratulations," he said flatly.

"You know what, Gabe, I don't have time for your pettiness right now. I have some celebrating to do." She actually planned to head back to her office and get some work done before leaving for the day. With Monday off, she looked forward to the three-day weekend. Vegging out in front of the television and binge-watching some legal thrillers, with wine and junk food being a part of her celebration.

Journey turned toward the stairs that would take her to their offices, but Gabe grabbed her arm, his hand firm with his keys digging into her skin.

"Ow," she flinched, stunned by his aggressiveness. "You're hurting me. Let go." When he tightened his hold, panic raced down her spine.

"I didn't like you when you first started in the DA's office, and I like you even less now."

"I suggest you release me or—"

"Or what? You'll call your boyfriend?" The menacing tone in his voice and the wicked leer in his eyes sent chills through her body. "I don't give a damn that you're sleeping with the cop, and I don't care that you've got the boss thinking that you're Ms. Perfect. You just need to know that I will destroy you if you get in my way of getting what I want."

Her initial shock now turned into anger. "Let. Me. Go," she ground out, wincing in pain as she twisted again in his grasp. "I said, let me go!" She lifted her knee toward his groin and just before making contact, Gabe blocked her movement with his free hand. His grip slacked enough for her to get out of his hold, but he didn't back away.

"You better be careful. You're starting to act more and more like your man. If you keep hanging around with scum, you're going to lose everything you've worked for."

Breathing hard, she rubbed her arm. "I don't know what you're talking about, but I bet you'd like it if I failed, wouldn't you? Since you can't become lead prosecutor on your own merit, you'd be next in line if I fall from grace."

"Now you listen here. I—"

"No, *you* listen," she hissed, so mad she felt like slapping him. Instead she jabbed his chest with her finger, ignoring the attention they had attracted.

"Don't you ever step to me the way you just did. And if you put your hands on me again, you'll be the one needing a lawyer. Keep harassing me and the restraining order that I'm thinking about filing against you will be the least of your problems. Now stay the hell away from me."

Journey walked away on shaky legs, but with her head held high. No way would she allow him to see how much the encounter had shaken her. She had threatened him with a restraining order, but now that he'd gotten physical, she might have to see the threat through.

When she made it back to their suite of offices, Journey stormed past her assistant Casey and headed for her office, still in shock at Gabe's behavior. She'd had just about enough of him and was thinking more and more about filing harassment charges. But she didn't want to come across as a crybaby, screaming harassment so soon after being appointed assistant district attorney.

No, there had to be something else she could do.

"Can I talk to you?" Casey asked as she followed closely behind Journey.

"Not now, Casey," Journey responded more harshly than she intended, but didn't stop to apologize. She marched into her office and slammed the door behind her.

Dropping her bag into one of the guest chairs, she paced the length of the room, her heels silent against the cheap carpet, her pulse pounding loudly in her ear. She should be celebrating a win; instead, she was trying to calm her frayed nerves and figure out what to do about Gabe.

She glanced down at her arm where he had grabbed her. Even with her dark skin, the area was red and a key imprint stood out like florescent pink against a brown backdrop.

"He's going to regret putting his hands on me," she ground out and went back to pacing. Her heart was still pounding a staccato rhythm when someone knocked on her door before it flew open.

"Journey, I'm sorry, he just barged passed me saying he needed to see you about a search warrant," Casey said after Laz walked in as if he had a right to do so. Casey's eyes shot daggers at his back, but Laz didn't seem to care. His piercing eyes bored into Journey like scorching rays from the sun, pinning her in place as warmth spread through her body.

Occasionally, his penetrating gaze made her antsy, but not today. Today butterflies fluttered wildly in her stomach at the sight of him. She hadn't seen Laz in well over a week, and she'd be lying if she didn't admit she was happy to see him now.

Wait. He shouldn't be here.

Casey cleared her throat and Journey's gaze shot to her assistant, whose raised brow was loaded with questions.

"It's all right, Casey. I can take it from here."

She hesitated, but eventually closed the door. Without diverting his attention from her, Laz backed up to the door and turned the lock.

"Laz, what are you doing here?" she asked quietly. Her office wasn't soundproof, but it still offered somewhat of a buffer to those nearby. More than that, the DA's office was the last place he should be.

"What's with the attitude? Bad day?" He watched her. The intensity in his stare dug deep into her soul as if he was trying to read her.

Journey turned to the tall bookshelf that held volumes of her law books, framed certificates and awards. She had worked hard to get where she was today, but the items on display did nothing to soothe her frustration. "The day started out great. I won th—"

"The McNealy case," Laz finished. She glanced over her shoulder and the corner of his lips lifted slightly before he said, "Congratulations. I had no doubt you could win."

"You were there?"

"I was at the courthouse for another trial."

"Oh." She turned back to the bookshelf and rubbed her neck.

The argument with Gabe returned to the forefront of her mind. She knew going into law that she would have to overcome challenges. Dealing with a few arrogant male attorneys over the years who tried to make her feel inferior happened more often than not. Yet, the situation with Gabe had her stumped. What was his problem? Journey could speculate, but...

Laz touched her hand and she startled, jerking away from his touch. He had moved from across the room without her realizing it.

He narrowed his eyes at her before reaching for her hand again. His touch was gentle, but something was off about him today. Journey couldn't quite put her finger on it, but he seemed edgier than usual. His face revealed nothing, though.

"Tell me what's going on with you and that asshole Hall."

Journey's eyebrows lifted in shock. "You saw what happened?" she asked just above a whisper.

*

"Yeah," Laz said absently, examining her arm.

He had almost lost his shit when he saw Gabe grab her. The pained expression on her face had been like a knife piercing his heart. The only thing that stopped him from going to her aid was that she had gotten the situation under control with a move that had surprised him. Besides that, he knew if he had approached them, he'd be in jail for assault.

Still looking at her arm, Laz froze. "That bastard grabbed you hard enough to leave a bruise?" He tried bridling the rage in his voice, but even he recognized the hardness in his tone. His anger spiked when he touched the darkened area and she flinched.

Gabriel Hall had just earned himself an ass-whoopin'.

"It's fine, Laz." Journey eased her arm out of his grasp.

"I bruise easily, and I can handle Gabe."

"You shouldn't have to *handle* him, Journey. He shouldn't have had his fucking hands on you!"

"Laz, I'm not helpless. I handled the situation and it's done. So drop it. And why are you so upset?"

"Damn it, Journey! That fuc—" He stopped himself, trying to rein in the rage hurtling through his body. "I don't want *any* man's hands on you!"

Her mouth dropped open at his fierce revelation. The admission surprised even him, but he meant it.

"Do you have any idea how hard it was for me not to snatch him up and strangle his ass? It's bad enough to know that men are putting their hands on women to inflict harm, but when that woman is you..." he choked out, emotion clogging his throat. Closing his eyes, he scrubbed his hands down his face.

He didn't bother finishing. He had already said too much.

Laz didn't want to admit that over the years she had somehow earned a spot in his heart. He didn't know when it happened, but he could no longer deny his feelings; at least not to himself.

That didn't mean he had any intention of acting on those feelings. Then again, he was powerless to stay away from her.

Chapter Seven

A part of Journey wanted Laz to finish what he was saying, but the other part of her was glad he hadn't. They couldn't pursue a relationship. Yet, when he spoke like that, with so much potency, that's exactly what she wanted.

But the two of them together wouldn't be a good idea. She knew it and he knew it. They didn't fit. He was a rule-breaker, toeing the line of justice while her moral compass kept her on a straight and narrow path.

But knowing those things didn't negate the fact that she wanted him more than she had ever wanted another man in her life.

Her heart rate amped up at the thought. Could she take a chance, ignore all common sense and lure this sexy, virile man into her bed? She had always enjoyed sex, especially when it was good. And she had a feeling that she and Laz would be better than just good together.

"Don't look at me like that, Journey."

"Like wh-what?" She wiped her sweaty palms down the sides of her dark skirt as Laz approached her, his steps measured.

She stood perfectly still while he zoned in on her mouth as if he wanted to kiss her. Or maybe that was wishful thinking on her part, since she would love to kiss him again.

Instead, she'd had to rely on memories of their last one, as well as the steamy dreams she'd been having about him lately. The ones that had her waking up every morning sexually frustrated.

Laz stopped in front of her, staring in that way he did so often with those seductive eyes of his. Instead of kissing her like she wanted, he cupped her cheek, brushing his thumb lightly over her skin, sending goose bumps up her arm, and lust rushing through her body. He could be so sweet and gentle at times.

"I don't like it when anyone hurts you."

Again, the possessiveness in his tone, like moments ago, spoke volumes. But what was she supposed to say to that?

Seconds ticked by with them staring into each other's eyes, but then his mouth covered hers, his kiss hungry and demanding. His strong arm went around her waist, drawing her closer to his muscular body and an electrical charge shot to the soles of her feet. Their tongues tangled and heat spread through her veins like a ferocious fire.

Journey had never felt so out of control, not even with Tony, but that's how it was with Laz lately. The delicious assault of his mouth against hers made her feel so desired. Like he craved her as much as she longed for him.

And this kiss... This was more than a kiss. He was claiming her, but that couldn't be right. He knew they couldn't be together. Didn't he?

How was she supposed to keep a level head when he kissed like he invented the act? And being wrapped in his arms had her body melting against him. It was a good thing he held her close because his kiss was siphoning all of her strength and she could barely stand.

Laz backed her to the wall, pulling the tail of her blouse out of her skirt. Without missing a beat, he quickly unbuttoned the garment and his warm hand slid up her torso. Journey whimpered when he ran his thumb over the lace of her bra. Her nipples pebbled from his scorching touch, and her breasts begged to be free.

"Laz," she breathed, her eyes closed and the back of her head brushed back and forth against the wall when he buried his face against the crook of her neck. Kissing. Nipping. Licking her heated skin. His hands moved slowly down her body, and she tingled everywhere his lips and fingers touched.

He unfastened the front clasp of her bra with a flick of his wrist, and her breasts spilled out into his palms.

"Journey," he murmured against her lips, his voice husky and filled with pent-up need as he caressed her. He pulled back slightly and glanced down at her. "Damn, you're even more beautiful than I imagined."

Waves of pleasure rocked through Journey while he admired her body. Her panties were already wet and she was more than ready as he salivated at her breasts as if they were chocolate-covered strawberries. When his mouth returned to hers, she moaned at the way he palmed her mounds, squeezing and teasing her sensitive peaks.

Journey's hands went to his hair, her fingers fisting the silky strands as she held on while she succumbed to the forceful domination of his lips. He moaned and ripped his mouth from hers, mumbling something in a language she didn't recognize. Was that Greek? She wasn't sure but before she could form her next thought, he took one of her nipples into his mouth.

Her skin prickled with the heat from his lips and her knees went weak. Laz slid an arm to her waist as he continued the sweet torture, cupping one of her breasts in his large hand. His tongue, teasing, licking, and swirling around her nipple. A moan of ecstasy slipped from her lips.

She couldn't breathe.

She couldn't think straight.

And she wanted him like a thirsty woman wanted a cold glass of water.

Laz went lower, trailing feathery kisses down the center of her breasts, and continued south, lingering around her navel.

This man... Lord, this man. She wanted this. She wanted

him. But one of them had to be smart. One of them had to keep their relationship professional. When he cupped and squeezed her breasts again, she groaned and knew she couldn't be the smart one.

As soon as the thought crossed her mind, his phone vibrated.

No! No! No!

Laz didn't stop, but disappointment slammed into Journey when the device vibrated again. The humming filled the quietness of the office, effectively bringing them back to reality.

"Shit!" The word flew from his mouth in a hoarse whisper and then he growled. Now on his knees in front of her, he dropped his forehead against her belly.

Journey wasn't sure if he was cursing because of the interruption or because they had gone further than they should. Had his phone not vibrated, there was no telling what they would've done in her office.

And knowing she had no intention of stopping him, Journey questioned her sanity.

She stared at the ceiling, her head against the wall while her breathing slowly returned to normal. Laz still had his head on her belly and her fingers sifted slowly through his thick hair, a calm settling over her. He didn't bother checking his phone and they stayed that way for the longest time until he stood to his full height.

Eyes half-closed and his hands on her waist, his gaze took in her nudity. He didn't speak as seconds ticked by, but his touch against her bare torso sent tingles racing across her skin. Maybe she should've been embarrassed, still standing before him with her clothes hanging off. She couldn't explain it, but she felt totally comfortable in front of him.

Even so, she fastened her bra and started to pull her blouse closed before Laz stopped her with his hand on her wrist. He then surprised the heck out of her when he started rebuttoning her blouse. There was a certain intimacy that went along with the gesture that made her heart melt a little bit.

"I owe you an apology." He cupped her face between his large hands and kissed her sweetly. Considering how gruff he usually was, his tenderness with her was palpable. "I—I lost control."

"Maybe, but I'm glad you did."

"Yeah, but this… Baby, you and I together, probably not a good move," he rasped.

"I know," Journey said reluctantly knowing he was right, but trying to fight the sweet thrill swirling in her stomach at the term of endearment he'd just used.

He eased away from her and she dropped down in her office chair while he adjusted his clothing and moved to the front of her desk.

She lifted the collar of her blouse and shook it, trying to cool herself off. Each look, each touch and each kiss from him made her crave him that much more.

Neither of them spoke for a long time, probably thinking the same thing and knowing if they kept this behavior up things could really get out of hand. They could ruin their professional relationship.

Laz cleared his throat and caught her attention. "Tell me what happened between you and Hall."

Journey thought for a moment. "I'm not sure, Laz. Something is going on with him, and I think it's more than just him being jealous of my promotion."

Laz folded his thick arms across his chest, his muscles bunching under his light blue dress shirt. She liked when he wore a suit, though right now he didn't have his suit jacket on. And he had probably loosened his paisley tie the moment he stepped out of the court room. He looked good in whatever he wore, but his normal attire was a T-shirt and jeans when on duty.

"What did he say to you in the hallway?"

Journey shook her head and pulled her attention from Laz's enticing body. He could be seriously intense sometimes when discussing a case, but the vibe she was getting from him at the moment was more aggressive than usual.

"Gabe is under the impression that you and I are sleeping together."

Laz's brows drew into a frown. "What's it to him if we were? Does he have a thing for you or something?"

"No, he hates me and this isn't the first time he's brought you up in conversation. He also mentioned that I'd better stay out of his way or else. On that I have no idea what he's talking about."

"That asshole threatened you?" Laz growled and when she didn't respond right away, he placed his hands palms down on her desk. "Journey?"

She didn't answer the question; instead she said, "He wants to be an assistant DA or who knows, maybe even DA. Gabe has been here longer than me and feels slighted that I received a promotion over him."

Laz blew out a noisy breath, still looking a little tense. "I should have beat his ass when I had a chance."

"I'm glad you didn't. Assaulting a government official is a federal offense." Besides, he'd been in enough trouble. He didn't need anything else to spotlight his already shaky reputation.

"Does that mean you're going to press charges against him?"

Stunned by the question, Journey said nothing, but he was right. She needed to do something.

"I'll take your silence as a no."

"I've got this, Laz, but thanks for caring."

"I care more than you know," he mumbled under his breath. "Has Hall ever put his hands on you before?"

"No."

"Good. Stay away from him. And if he even acts like he wants to touch you again, let me know."

"Laz," she dragged out his name. "Stay out of this. Don't do anything that's going to draw more attention on you."

"Hey, I'm not going to touch the guy as long as he doesn't touch you." He started for the door, but stopped suddenly as if just remembering something. Crossing the room, he walked around the desk and stood next to her chair. "Are you ready to tell me what's going on around here that involves me?"

"Yes," she said without hesitation. It was time she told him what she knew. "But not here."

"Then where and when?"

"I'll text you."

"If I don't hear from you soon, you'll be hearing from me." He moved toward the office door, and she hated to see him leave.

"Oh, Laz, wait. I forgot to ask. What's this about you needing help getting a warrant?"

He smirked, smiling for the first time since arriving. That bad-boy grin always made her off-balance. "I just said that to get in here."

He opened the door but turned back to her. "I'll be in touch."

Chapter Eight

An hour later, Laz found a parking spot around the corner from Club Masquerade, the hottest night club in Atlanta. He really wasn't in the mood for large crowds, but had agreed to meet his best friend, Hamilton Crosby, for a drink.

Laz laid his head against the headrest and stared out his front windshield at nothing in particular. He still couldn't shake what he'd witnessed between Hall and Journey. Nor could he stop thinking about what happened in her office. He'd gone too far and the scary part was, she hadn't stopped him. The instant his lips touched her body, he knew he had screwed up because he wanted more of her.

Much more.

Groaning, he sat up and patted his pockets for the pack of cigarettes as well as the burner phone he had picked up a short while ago. Knowing he had both, he climbed out of his old Chevy, cringing at how loud the creaky driver's side door was when he opened it. One day soon he was going to have to break down and go car shopping.

Before heading around the corner to the club, he stopped and leaned his back against a building, his right foot propped on the brick. Tapping out a cigarette from the pack of smokes, he lit it and relaxed a little after the first puff.

When he had quit smoking several years ago, he had no intention of picking up the bad habit again, but a five-day suspension a few months ago had changed that.

He didn't smoke often. These days, a pack of cigarettes usually lasted a few weeks, but tonight he was horny as hell and walking around with a semi-erection. If he couldn't have the woman he wanted, he'd have to settle for a smoke.

He took a long drag on the cigarette and released a thin cloud of smoke into the atmosphere, as he zoned in on three women who were approaching. One of them was pointing at something on her cell phone, while the other two peered over her shoulder at the screen. The woman closest to the street, a redhead who stood almost a foot taller than the other two, glanced at him and smiled. Laz gave her a head nod, but said nothing when they passed by.

He'd never had a problem attracting women, but after losing Gwenn years ago, he had changed, becoming a hit-it-and-quit-it kind of guy. He might've had a couple of fuck buddies, but nothing serious, especially in the last six months.

But now Journey was on his radar and he wasn't quite sure what to do with his feelings for her. Hell, he couldn't even pinpoint when their attraction had grown more intense.

She should've pushed me away.

Getting adjusted to her new role in the district attorney's office, and knowing that he was constantly under scrutiny in his department and now hers, Journey had more to lose than him. He wouldn't be able to forgive himself if he did anything to soil her reputation. And he had no intention of letting anyone else hurt her either. Namely Hall.

Laz pushed away from the building and took one last puff on his cigarette before putting it out. He needed to take care of Hall, make sure he thought twice about putting his hands on any woman.

Pulling the burner phone from his pocket, Laz stepped into the shadows of a storefront that was closed and dialed a number he used for special occasions.

"Yeah, who dis?" The gruff voice on the other end

answered.

"It's me. I need a favor."

Laz was met with silence at first. "I think you've used up all of your favors, detective."

"You think so?" Laz asked, his tone deadly, not in the mood for bullshit.

He had helped this guy out of more jams of the criminal nature than he could count. The last time was keeping his little brother out of jail. Laz knew he'd need his contact's special services one day, and this was one of those times he was glad he knew people in low places.

After a long pause, his contact asked, "Whatcha need?"

"I need you to pay someone a visit. Someone who roughed up a woman."

"Damn, man. Should've started with that. You know how I feel about assholes who abuse women."

Laz gave him the information he'd gathered on Gabriel Hall, as well as instructed him where he could find a photo of the guy. "Be sure to do some major damage to his face, but don't kill him and don't get caught."

His contact grunted. As if him getting caught was a joke.

"Let me put it a different way," Laz continued. "If you get caught, you're on your own."

He disconnected and walked around the corner, tossing the phone into a sewer drain along the way. The last thing he needed was to have anything linking him to the ass-whoopin' Hall had coming.

Fifteen minutes later, Laz brought his beer bottle to his lips and took a healthy gulp as he scanned Club Masquerade's rooftop deck. Standing at a tall cocktail table, he had a good view of the city as well as the patrons. Some danced to the latest song by Drake while others drank, laughed, and chatted at tables set up around the large space. Considering the day had been in the high eighties, it had cooled significantly. But that didn't stop the scantily-clad women from strutting around as if it was ninety degrees outside.

"Here you go, love." A server set another beer on the

table.

"I didn't order that." Laz slid the bottle toward her. He was off duty, but rarely did he consume more than one beer while out.

"The redhead over there ordered it for you." She gestured with a nod to the group of women sitting two tables away that Laz had seen earlier.

"All right, thanks." He lifted the bottle in salute to the woman who was now smiling at him. He had a type. Red fit the look with her cute face, curvaceous body and long, shapely legs. That's what he'd remembered most about her from when he saw her outside minutes ago.

Eyeing her now, she was definitely pretty, but he felt nothing. No desire to kiss her. No desire to have her in his bed. No desire to have those long legs wrapped around his waist. Nothing. And he knew why.

Journey. The woman had ruined him for others and he hadn't even gotten her into bed yet.

"And I never will," he mumbled, mentally reminding himself of why.

"I see you haven't lost your touch."

Laz glanced over his shoulder and then stood as Hamilton sidled up next to him. They shook hands and exchanged a one-armed hug, pounding each other on the back.

"You've only been here a few minutes and already women are buying you drinks."

"Hey, I didn't initiate the attention."

"Yeah, you rarely do," Hamilton grunted and accepted a ginger ale from the same server. "It's those damn eyes. I guess they're still working for you."

Laz grinned. "Don't hate, man. I can't help it if the female gender finds me irresistible."

"Yeah, whatever."

Hamilton Crosby was not only Laz's best friend, but he'd also been his college roommate at Georgia State. They both majored in criminology and upon graduating from college, had joined Atlanta's police force. Hamilton had left the department years ago, and now was a managing partner of Supreme Security. It was a personal security agency that was quickly gaining notoriety across the country.

"So, what's going on with you?" Hamilton asked and sipped his drink, eyeing Laz skeptically.

"What? Can't a guy just call up his old pal to hang out?"

"Yeah, but usually that happens every couple of weeks for most people. I haven't heard from you in over a month. I had to call Ashton at the station to see if you were still alive. Where I come from, friends...brothers keep in touch, especially with the type of work we both do."

He was right. Neither of them were big phone people, but there was no excuse for not keeping in contact. There was a time when a week didn't go by that they didn't get together for a drink, shoot pool, or play poker.

"Sorry about that, man. Been doing a little undercover work and putting in some long hours. You know how it is." Laz shrugged. "These days I'm just trying to keep my head down and stay out of trouble."

"Because of a woman?"

Laz sputtered out his beer, coughing when the liquid went down wrong. "Nah, man. What's wrong with you? Nobody said anything about a woman. I've just been busy."

"If *you're* trying to stay out of trouble, there has to be a woman involved. And not just any woman. Someone who... Well, I'll be damned," Hamilton said, wonder in his voice. "It's serious, isn't it? You and the ADA. Is that why you finally called me back? You need to talk it out."

Laz sighed roughly and shook his head. "I'm not doing this with you tonight, Ham. So drop it. Just because you've found love doesn't mean it's in the cards for the rest of us. How is Dakota anyway?"

Hamilton had recently married Dakota Sherrod, a stuntwoman—well, *former* stuntwoman. After a serious accident, the adrenaline junky had given up her dangerous job and slowed down a little. Now she spent her days running a dojo, putting her black belt in karate to good use by teaching martial arts.

"Dakota is fine, and though she's still waiting for you to RSVP to our wedding reception invitation, I told her to count you in."

Laz nodded. "I'll be there."

"I take it the new ADA has seriously gotten to you, huh? Let me guess, you're tired of fighting the attraction."

Laz looked at him in amazement. There were advantages to having friends who knew you well, but those same advantages could also be disadvantages. Like now. His friend still had the ability to read him.

"What? Don't look so surprised. You forget, I know you. Besides, this past year you've found a way to bring her name into every conversation. It was only a matter of time that you stepped to her."

"I haven't stepped to her." Well, not exactly, Laz thought silently.

"If that's true, then maybe you should. Because right now you're wound tighter than a bowline knot. Why not just hit that and—"

"Chill, man. She's not that type of woman," he practically growled, unable to keep the irritation from his voice. He'd admit, when it came to women, he wasn't the lovey-dovey-dating type of guy, but if he had Journey, he had a feeling it would be different.

No, he knew it would be different.

Hamilton remained silent before saying, "Should I tell Dakota to put you down for a plus-one regarding the reception? I know Journey means something to you. If—"

"Whether she does or not, nothing's going to happen between us. She and I..." Laz shook his head without finishing. He needed to keep reminding himself why it wasn't a good idea to get involved with her.

"I've never known you to back down from something you want, especially when it comes to women. Why now?"

Laz released a humorless laugh. "You have to ask? Man,

I'm a fuck-up. The last thing she needs is someone who'll tarnish her life, or worse, get her killed. Nah, I'm keeping my distance."

"You did not get Gwenn killed."

"Didn't I? If it weren't for my need for justice, Gwenn would still be alive. Now I'm done talking about Journey, Gwenn, and women period. I just came here to have a drink and catch up with you. That's it."

"Fine, for now. But I'm not done questioning you about that fine ADA."

Laz chuckled and shook his head, knowing this conversation was far from over. Back in his cop days, Hamilton had been a beast when it came to interrogating a perp, always getting the answers he wanted.

For the next hour, they talked, catching up on each other's lives. Hearing about his godson's latest shenanigans had Laz laughing out loud. Dominic, Hamilton's son, a kid who was easy to love with his sharp mind, intuition, and ability to be funny without trying, was the son Laz wished he had.

Conversation continued to flow easily as they talked sports, something Laz didn't get to watch as often as he'd like, and then they discussed work. He found it refreshing to talk about some of his cases with someone who could understand the frustration of the job. He also knew he didn't have to worry about anything he said getting out to anyone else.

"Why are you still on the force?" Hamilton asked after silence fell between them. "I can tell your heart isn't in it anymore. Between the IA investigations and suspensions, I have to ask. Why keep putting up with the bullshit?"

Lately, Laz had been asking himself the same question. There was a time that he loved his job. Granted, there were other jobs he could do using his current skills and his degree, but taking out bad guys was what he knew.

His attention went back to the people on the rooftop. Club Masquerade was owned by the Bennett triplets who had inherited the business from their parents a few years ago. It was a good gig they had going and within a short amount of time, they'd made the club into a hot spot for not just those who were local, but for those visiting the city as well.

"How do you like working for Mason Bennett?" Laz asked Hamilton. Mason was not only part owner of the club, but also part owner of Supreme Security Agency-Atlanta.

"It's cool, man. I'm only at the club occasionally now that Supreme is growing."

The agency, which offered protection for entertainers, corporations, and government agencies, had grown to the point of almost doubling its clientele list within the last year. Hamilton played a big role in that, proving that the position with the company suited him. And now that he was married, Laz had noticed he even seemed happier...and more settled.

Feelings Laz had been longing for recently.

"You know, if you're ever looking for a change of pace, Mase is always in the market for a few good people," Hamilton said. "A chunk of his team is made of Atlanta's finest, and you and I both know you're the best there is."

Laz chuckled. "Flattery. Wow."

"Hey, I'm just telling the truth. You work for Atlanta PD. Bust your ass daily to wipe the streets clean of scumbags and where has it gotten you? Most of them might spend a few years behind bars, but many are back on the streets before you can even collar the next crook."

"Don't remind me," Laz grunted, finishing off his second beer and handing the empty bottle to a server walking by. "Seems the harder I work, the tougher it is to get a conviction. Most days I feel like I'm wasting my time."

"Like I asked before. Why are you still there?"

"If not me out here, then who, Ham? The streets are getting worse by the day. That's where I'm needed. Besides, I can't let what happened to Gwenn happen to anyone else."

Hamilton shook his head. "Laz, you're just one person. You can't do it alone. Besides, you took care of Ray and the Apostle Kings. You got justice for her death. It's time to move on."

They'd had similar conversations on occasion for the last nine years. From the moment Laz found her dead in their house, a needle filled with heroin lying next to her, he'd been on a mission. Not many days went by that he didn't relive that dark time of his life.

"I don't know if I'll ever be able to let those memories go."

"Yeah, I know, but even if you can't let the memories go, you can leave the job behind. Actually, it might do you some good to finally start fresh and make some changes in your life."

Hamilton's mention of making changes made Laz immediately think of Journey. Could he change? Could he turn his life and reputation around and possibly be the type of man to get and keep a woman like her?

Hamilton pulled out his wallet and a card, then handed it to Laz. "You can make twice as much money providing personal security as you make on the force. When you're ready to move on, give Mason a call. I know he has a spot for you."

Laz skimmed the business card. *Supreme Security Agency* in gold lettering at the top and Mason Bennett's contact information below it. Laz had done well for himself financially, living below his means and investing most of his salary. But making more money definitely wouldn't be a bad thing.

This wasn't the first time Hamilton had tried recruiting him, but it was the first time Laz was seriously considering joining the team.

Laz's cell phone vibrated in his pocket. A quick glance at the screen and a twinge of anticipation gripped him. A text from Journey.

Can you meet me in thirty minutes?

Little did she know he'd meet her anytime anywhere for anything. He typed a quick response.

Just say where. I'll be there.

After getting her response, he stood. "Ham, it's been real, but I gotta go. If you're cool with it, let Dom know he and I are hanging out tomorrow night. I've missed my little buddy."

"All right, and it might not hurt to get his opinion on Journey. Dakota insists that it was because of the kid that she gave me a shot.

Laz chuckled, remembering how Dominic acquired Dakota's phone number when he and Hamilton first met her on a movie set. His godson had recently turned ten, but acted as if he was twenty years older. A good judge of character, Dominic was a charmer. Women fell in love with him immediately and the kid had made a good wingman for Laz in the past.

Yeah, maybe he would introduce Dom to Journey one day.

"It was good seeing you, man," Hamilton said, following Laz to the stairs that led back into the main part of the club. "And think about what I said. It might be time for a change."

"I hear you." It was definitely time for a change and for the first time in a long time, Laz looked forward to his future.

Chapter Nine

A half an hour later, Laz sat at Journey's breakfast bar with a hot cup of coffee, trying to make sense of what she was telling him.

Maybe his brain was tired since it was almost eleven-thirty and it had been an exhausting day. Normally, when he stopped by a woman's house this time of night it was a booty call, but he kept reminding himself that this was Journey. And this was business.

"Journey, if you're talking about internal affairs, IA has been busting my ass for years. I can handle them, and I hate that's what's been bothering you."

When she had first told him to watch his back—something he always did—Laz hadn't been sure what to think. He'd admit to being sick of IA harassing him, but they didn't dish out anything he wasn't used to.

"Laz, that's not it. I—I heard the DA's office is investigating you and one of your cases."

Unease crept up his back and the coffee cup stalled near his mouth before he slowly lowered it to the counter. Questions ran rampant through his mind and he wasn't sure which ones to ask first. Being investigated by IA was one thing, but being investigated by her office was on a different level.

"Laz…"

"What case?" he asked, a little harsher than intended.

She hesitated and pulled her lower lip between her teeth. He knew he was asking a lot, assuming whatever was going on was in the early stages. But Laz needed as much information as possible to prepare himself for whatever was coming.

"Journey, I need you to tell me everything you can. I promise you, it stops right here."

"I heard that our office is reopening the Monsuli case because…the DA was informed that some of the evidence had been planted."

"What? That's bullshit!" He leaped from the barstool, startling her. "So all of a sudden they decide the evidence is no good? I'm not buying that."

"Monsuli's lawyer is trying to get the original case overturned. If that happens—"

"Monsuli walks," Laz finished, annoyance roaring through his body. He ran his hand over his mouth and paced near the kitchen. Memories of that arrest and the hours afterward floated to the front of his mind.

"They think you planted evidence, Laz."

"I'll admit, I've done some dirty shit over the years, but I wouldn't intentionally jeopardize my case."

Journey said nothing and anxiousness twisted in Laz's gut. Did she believe him? Even if there could never be anything between them, what she thought of him mattered.

"Anyone who really knows me knows that I'd do almost anything to put a criminal away, especially if I knew without a doubt that they were guilty. But this…"

Journey exhaled loudly as if she'd been holding her breath. "I know, and I believe you had nothing to do with tainted evidence. But Laz, this is serious. Depending on what comes of the investigation, the DA can press charges. You could do time."

He just stared at her. He had busted his ass for the city for the last seventeen years, and he'd be damned if he went to jail for some shit like this.

"This guy can't go free. Do you remember three years ago, six teenagers were found shot dead under the Buford Highway bridge?"

"I remember."

"That was Monsuli's doing. Those kids were drug runners for him and had started using his merchandise. We could never get enough evidence to formally charge him or anyone in his camp. I can give you a handful of other instances off the top of my head where he was involved. And finally, we catch him, with a murder weapon, and you're telling me he might walk. What type of sense does that make?"

"Laz, I know the legal system can be frustrating, but it works. We can't keep him in jail unless we know for sure he did the crime we're charging him for."

"What evidence are they claiming was planted?" he asked, his anger almost at its tipping point.

"The knife used to kill the victim. It has the vic's blood on it, and according to forensics, Monsuli's prints aren't on the weapon. Yours are."

Laz's mouth gaped open. "That's crazy!" Even if he was going to plant evidence, there's no way he'd be sloppy about it.

"Monsuli insists you're trying to frame him since you haven't been able to get anything on him in the past."

"I caught the bastard with the knife in his hand, Journey. He wasn't wearing gloves. When I ordered him to freeze, he dropped the weapon to the floor."

"Then what did you do with the knife?"

Laz didn't forget details of a case, especially this one.

The drug kingpin, a supplier of heroin, meth, and cocaine, had been on Laz's radar for years, but they could never nail him. A few years ago, when one of his customers ended up dead, they thought they had him, but one of his minions took the fall, admitting to first-degree murder.

"There's no way my prints are on that weapon. I had the

responding officers tag it for evidence."

She didn't speak, only stared at him with her big brown doe-like eyes that were filled with sympathy. He didn't want her pity. All he wanted was to get to the bottom of whatever this nonsense was.

"Whatever they think they have on me is bullshit. Either they have the wrong knife, or somebody is trying to set *me* up. Either way, I'm not taking this shit sitting down."

He headed to the door, but Journey caught up to him and grabbed his arm.

"You can't say anything about all of this yet, Laz. I probably shouldn't have even told you since I could lose my job if it got back to my office that I shared confidential information. But…I owe you."

He knew exactly what she was referring to, and over the years, memories of that night filtered into his mind. She didn't know this, but since the night she'd almost been raped, he had kept tabs on her. She still worked late hours, which he hated, but at least now she didn't use public transportation at night. She had started either driving or ordering a car to get home from work.

Laz still got the shakes whenever he thought about the night she'd been attacked. The situation could've gone very different had he not happened to be in the area and heard her screaming.

"Baby, you don't owe me anything, especially where *that* night is concerned. I'm glad I was there for you." He caressed her delicate cheek, loving the way her eyes drifted closed as she leaned into his touch.

What the hell was he going to do about this woman? This adorable, intelligent woman who dominated so many of his thoughts.

Her eyes fluttered open again, and his hand slid behind her neck, pulling her closer. He wanted to kiss her sweet lips again, wanted just a little taste of her delectable mouth. All it would take was for him to lean down slightly, especially considering how willing she seemed.

Staring into her troubled eyes, he held onto her, his thumb caressing the soft skin beneath her ear.

"Thanks for the heads-up. I swear to you, I won't say a word."

He lowered his head, inches from her mouth, but at the last minute settled for kissing her on the forehead. If he had kissed her lips, there was no way he'd be able to leave without stripping her out of her clothes and taking her body the way he'd desired.

"Lock up, and I'll see you around."

Laz stood on the other side of the door until he heard the lock click into place before strolling to the elevator. He knew he was going to regret not kissing her, not holding her close to his body and feeling her softness against him. But he had to walk away.

He had to figure out how to leave her alone without actually leaving her alone, because he already knew he didn't want to go too many days without seeing her.

Just before pushing the down button for the elevator he stopped, his finger stalling in mid-air as he thought about Hamilton's words. His friend was right about one thing, Laz did always go after what he wanted and to hell with consequences.

But this situation was different. Journey was different...special. He'd never forgive himself if any of his actions somehow came back on her or if he ever did anything to hurt her.

Then again, what would it hurt to go on one date with her?

Laz released a slow, steadying breath as an idea bloomed in his mind. He wanted to spend a little time with the sexy prosecutor. He returned to her apartment door and knocked before he could talk himself out of doing what he was about to do.

The door swung open almost immediately. "Laz? What's going on?"

"How do you feel about wedding receptions?"

Her left brow lifted in amusement. "As long as it's not

67

mine, I'm fine with them."

Laz leaned against the doorframe with his arms folded across his chest. He studied her, surprised by her response but he decided not to question her about it at the moment.

"Well, I usually try to stay clear of prosecutors unless I have no other choice," he said, loving the way her eyes sparkled when she laughed. "This is one of those times where I have no other choice. I need a date. I'm not sure if you remember my friend Hamilton Crosby, but he recently got married. How about being my plus-one for the reception? There will be plenty of food, drinks, and dancing, and maybe even cake. You interested?"

Journey twisted her bottom lip between her teeth, studying Laz for the longest time before a slow smile spread across her gorgeous mouth. "Cake, huh? Who can say no to cake? When's the reception, and can you even dance?"

"Baby, I've got moves that will blow your mind."

Chapter Ten

"Whose car is this?" Dominic asked, when he climbed into Laz's new Nissan Maxima.

"Mine. I picked it up yesterday. You like it?"

Laz had been thinking about buying a new car for the last couple of years but hadn't taken the time to look for one. The day after Journey had agreed to be his date for the reception, he figured that was as good of a day as any. As far as he was concerned, she was too classy of a woman for him to have her riding around in his twenty-year-old Chevy.

"It's nice, but you shoulda got a Mustang like the one Dakota has," Dominic said, referring to his stepmother's vehicle. The woman was an adrenaline junkie who operated on one speed when it came to driving. Fast. She had the speeding tickets to prove it.

"Why'd you come pick me up so early?" Dominic asked as he fastened his seatbelt.

"This was the time your dad told me to pick you up."

Hamilton had called earlier that morning to see if Laz was available to pick up Dominic from a sleepover. "Besides, Dom, it's not that early. We only have a little over an hour to get there, and you know how this traffic can be."

"Yeah, but," he huffed out a breath, "I was winning Pokémon Duel for the *first time*." He spoke the words as if he couldn't believe it. "Now Johnathan's going to be bragging every time I see him, talking about how he can't be beat."

"Oh. Well, sorry to mess up your groove, but you don't want to be late for your dad's reception, do you?"

"I guess not," he muttered, still looking defeated as his lower lip stuck out. "I really didn't wanna go to this reception in the first place, but Dad said I'd better be there or else. Glad I only have to stay for the dinner part."

Laz chuckled as he drove out of the prestigious subdivision and headed to the highway. The first part of the reception was a sit-down dinner for family and close friends, while the second part of the event would be a party that would include Hamilton and Dakota's friends who weren't invited to the dinner.

"Well, I'm glad you were forced to attend because there's someone I want you to meet."

"Who?" Dominic pulled a handheld game console out of his backpack, a device he rarely left home without.

"A...friend." When Dominic didn't say anything, Laz glanced at him. "What? What's that look for?"

"Is it your girlfriend?"

"I didn't say it was a woman."

Dominic grunted and Laz could almost hear the wheels in the kid's brain turning. "It must be a girl...I mean, a woman. I can tell 'cause of the way you said *friend.*"

Laz tried to fight the smile threatening to break free at the way Dominic said *friend,* as if it was a dirty word that left a bad taste on his tongue. Laz couldn't wait until the kid got interested in girls. He was so going to give him a hard time.

"I didn't know you had a girlfriend."

"I don't. I told you she's a *friend.* We're on our way to pick her up now so she can go to the reception with us."

"Why?"

Laz glanced at Dominic, splitting his attention between him and the road. "Why what?"

"Why is she going with us if she's not your girlfriend?"

"Because..." Laz started, trying to find the right words to explain why he invited a woman, who he had never spent

70

time with outside of work until recently and who he wasn't dating, to a wedding reception.

"If she's not your girlfriend," Dominic continued, his thumbs working feverishly as he played the video game, "you must like her like a girlfriend."

"Well…yeah, I like her. Otherwise I wouldn't have asked her to come with us, but she's not my girlfriend. I just…like her."

Laz realized that his responses were like those of a middle-schooler who had a crush on the most popular girl in class. Why did he feel a need to reiterate the fact that he and Journey weren't an item?

"Can we stop by GameStop on the way to pick up your *friend*?"

Laz frowned. He was glad the kid had dropped the interrogation but surprised by the sudden shift in the conversation. "Dom, I just told you we needed to pick her up."

"I know, but since she's not your girlfriend, maybe she won't mind if we're a little late."

On that, Laz did laugh. *Kids.* "Dom, man, you have a lot to learn about women. There's no way she'd be okay with me picking her up late."

A short while later, Laz pulled into the circular drive in front of Journey's high-rise apartment building. Not much made him nervous, but a bout of anxiousness swirled inside of him. It had been three days since he had last seen her, and a day hadn't gone by that he hadn't questioned his decision to invite her to the reception. Not because he didn't want to spend time with her, but he knew from experience that some women got the wrong idea when a guy invited them to a wedding or wedding reception.

But this is Journey. She didn't seem the type. From what he knew of her, her career was her sole focus.

Laz parked on the side of the driveway. "Dom, hop in the backseat. I'll be right back."

"Okay.

Laz entered the building and had just stepped up to the concierge's desk when he spotted Journey exiting the elevator.

Wow.

He didn't think she could get any more gorgeous, but seeing her in the navy-blue short, one shoulder dress stole his breath from his lungs. He swallowed hard and his pulse amped up as Journey strolled toward him. Thanks to the tasteful side-split in the dress, a toned, bronze thigh peeked out with each long step she took. His gaze went lower.

Goodness. Those legs.

He gawked at her long shapely legs that tapered down to a pair of sky-high shoes that had a thin strap around her slim ankles. Forget taking her to the reception. He was tempted to carry her back upstairs, strip her bare, and have his way with her.

Shit. This was Journey Ramsey. Friend. Coworker. *Sort of.* Whatever she was, he shouldn't be thinking thoughts like that about her. This evening they would just be hanging out…getting to know each other better. Nothing else.

Laz unbuttoned his suit jacket and tugged on the collar of his dress shirt, suddenly finding it too tight for comfort.

"Considering the way you're checking me out, detective, you either like what you see or you don't approve of my outfit. Which is it? Do I need to go upstairs and change into something else?"

"Don't you dare," he growled, boldly slipping his hand around her narrow waist and pulling her close to his side. So much for keeping his hands to himself. She was too irresistible. "You're sexy as hell. I'm a little hesitant to take you out in public for fear I might have to kick some guy's ass for checking you out."

Journey released a lyrical laugh that only made him want her that much more. How the hell was he going to get through the evening without pulling her into the nearest cleaning closet or bathroom stall to have his way with her?

"You know, with this outfit you might outshine the

bride."

"Now, I doubt that, and I must say, you clean up well." With her sweet smile and the way she ran her hand down the front of his jacket, heat soared through Laz's body.

He had planned to be a perfect gentleman tonight. However, considering the steady beat of desire pulsing through his veins and the need to have his hands all over her luscious body, the night was going to be pure torture.

What have I gotten myself into?

Chapter Eleven

Journey released a shaky breath in an effort to slow her pounding heart. With a hand at the small of her back, sending delicious tingles spiraling through her body, Laz escorted her across the lobby. She hadn't been this nervous since the time she faced her first case in court, and even then she'd been prepared.

But nothing, not even the speech she had given herself while staring into her bathroom mirror moments ago, could've prepared her for the sight of seeing Laz looking absolutely delicious in all black.

At over six feet tall with wide shoulders and hair that always looked as if he ran his fingers through it too many times, he was truly a vision. Add those hypnotic hazel-green eyes and kissable lips, and a girl could lose her mind around him. He was just that good-looking. But throw in a black suit, with a black shirt underneath where the top three buttons were undone, showing a wisp of chest hair, and she was practically fanning herself to keep from hyperventilating.

It's Laz. We're just hanging out. No big deal, she reminded herself.

But who was she kidding? She was out with Lazarus Dimas—the hot detective who always had her female coworkers falling all over themselves whenever he stopped by the DA's office.

Nope, this was no ordinary date, and that became apparent when she spent hours in a department store trying to find a dress for the reception. Normally, she enjoyed shopping, could mall-hop for hours upon hours with the best of them and not grow tired. Today was different, though. Today she had the added stress of wanting to impress Laz. She'd had to find the perfect dress, and if his reaction upon seeing her was any indication, she had done well.

"I'm to the right," Laz said, interrupting her musing as they exited through the revolving door. He directed her to a sleek black car with chrome rims and windows so dark, she couldn't see inside the vehicle.

"Nice car. New?"

"Mmhm. I couldn't have you riding around in my old beater."

Journey stopped. "Laz, I hope you didn't go out and purchase a car just because of me."

He shrugged and moved her forward with a hand on her elbow. "Let's just say you were my motivation to do something I should've done years ago."

"Well, it's nice, but you do know that it's against the law in Atlanta to have window tint that dark, right?"

He flashed that crooked grin that always made her squeeze her legs tightly together to ward off the lustful throb between her thighs. Whew, this man. She'd been physically attracted to him from the moment they met, but this evening that attraction had reached new heights.

"Yeah, I think I did read that in one of the police manuals that are currently lining the bottom of my desk drawer. Surely you know by now that I'm not that good at following rules."

"Oh, I know oh too well. I just didn't realize that same rebellious attitude extended to your personal life, too."

With his hand sliding around her waist, he slowed, forcing her to also decrease her pace. "Does that scare you, counselor?" he whispered near her ear, his warm breath and deep baritone sending a powerful shiver shooting through her body.

"You might intimidate others, *detective*, but you don't scare me," she lied.

Truth was, he scared the hell out of her. Not because she thought he would do her harm. No, it had everything to do with the fact that she didn't trust herself to use good judgment when it came to him. There was just something about him that made her want to throw out caution and take a ride on the wild side.

"What took so long, Uncle Laz?" A cute kid with skin the color of caramel and dark serious eyes asked, his head sticking out of the window as he looked Journey up and down.

She glanced at Laz with raised brows. "Uncle Laz?" It was clear the two weren't biologically related, but the title had her curious.

"Journey, this is my impatient godson, Hamilton's son, Dominic. Dom, this is Ms. Ramsey."

"Hi," he said shyly, still eyeing her warily.

"Hi, Dominic. It's nice to meet you," she said, amused at how he studied her as if trying to memorize every detail of her face. Now that she thought about it, Journey had seen a similar expression on Laz a few times, which made meeting Dominic even more interesting. Maybe they spent a lot of time together.

She leaned closer to Laz to whisper in his ear. "He seems kind of intense."

He chuckled, casting a loving gaze at the little boy before returning his attention to her. "Let's just say he's ten going on thirty, and brace yourself, he's a thinker. We never know what's going to come out of his mouth."

Journey nodded as Laz opened the door for her. Once she was settled inside, he hurried around the vehicle and climbed in on the driver's side.

"So what have you guys been up to today?" She glanced between him and Dominic, who looked up at her before returning his attention to his game.

"I had to work earlier, and then I picked Dom up from one of his friend's house a few minutes ago."

"I was at a sleepover."

"Did you have a good time?" she asked.

"It was fun...until Uncle Laz showed up," he grumbled.

A huge grin spread across Laz's handsome face as he maneuvered through traffic. Clearly, he had no remorse for cutting his godson's fun short. "He's ticked that I interrupted a video game that he was playing and winning."

"Ah, I see. You couldn't wait until he was finished?"

Laz frowned. "I guess I could have, but—"

"Mrs. Fischer made us turn it off," Dominic volunteered. "We were supposed to be downstairs by the time Uncle Laz came, but..."

"So technically it wasn't my fault." Laz slammed on the brakes. "Motherfu..." he started before catching himself and glanced in the rear-view mirror at Dominic, who laughed.

"Dad said Uncle Laz is trying to stop swearing, but he's not doing a good job."

Journey smiled. "Is that right?"

Laz said nothing as he switched lanes, mumbling something under his breath as he zoomed past the driver who was giving him grief, but Dominic continued.

"Yes, but Dee said it's a part of who Uncle Laz is, and he should be true to himself. Whatever that means."

"I liked that woman from day one," Laz added.

Journey laughed, already enjoying Dominic and the way that he and Laz interacted. She had a feeling that if she wanted to know any secrets about Laz, his godson would be the best source for information.

Listening as Laz and Dominic discussed Dakota, it was plain to see that they were both fond of her. It was also clear that Laz and Dominic had a special bond. The way they argued good-naturedly, finished each other's sentences and even their facial expression let her know they spent a lot of time together.

Spending time with Laz outside of the confines of their jobs was already enlightening. He was known for his bad boy-take-no-crap behavior, but his interaction with his godson revealed a different side of him. A gentler side.

"Your perfume is kind of strong," Dominic blurted out.

"Dom!" Laz said, and Journey sat stunned as she fought the laughter bubbling inside of her.

"What did I tell you about voicing the first thing that pops into your head, especially if it's not nice?" Laz admonished.

"What? It is strong, but at least it smells good," Dominic mumbled, his fingers tapping away on the video game in his hand as if he hadn't just insulted her.

"Thanks...I think," Journey said. "I'll try not to put so much on the next time."

She bit down on her bottom lip to keep from bursting out laughing. The last thing she wanted to do was undermine Laz's reprimand by falling out into a fit of giggles, but the comment had been funny. Apparently, Laz didn't think so though, if his deep frown and the strong set of his jaw were any indication.

Journey wasn't around kids much since she didn't know many people with little ones and most of her friends and her sister were focused on building their careers. So she didn't know if this was normal behavior for a ten-year-old. Yet Dominic and this situation was the perfect example of—*kids say the darnedest things.*

When they finally arrived at the hotel where the reception was being held, Dominic spotted his grandparents in the lobby and took off in a sprint toward them.

"That kid acts as if he has to run everywhere he goes," Laz said and waved at the older couple before directing Journey toward the ballroom. "And sorry about the whole perfume thing. If it makes you feel any better, I think you smell amazing," he said close to her ear with his arm around her waist. Clearly, he had no idea the effect he had on her when he was so close.

"Um...thank you. I actually thought it was funny. I like a man who speaks his mind."

The left side of Laz's mouth kicked up into a grin. "Good to know. Let's head inside. Dinner is scheduled to be served in about twenty minutes. Would you like something to drink in the meantime?"

"No, actually I'm good right now. This room is beautiful," she said, admiring the intimate space that was classily decorated in mostly white with teal accents. White gossamer fabric covered the walls and looped intricately from the ceilings, creating an elegant ambiance. A sweet melody floated through the room from the band that was set up on the far side of the room with their lead singer

Her gaze traveled around the room, noting the attention they were garnering from people who were standing around and others who were already occupying some of the tables. Journey wasn't one to shrink inside herself when people stared, but she couldn't help wonder if they were looking at them because they made a striking couple. Or if it had more to do with the fact that they were a mixed-race couple. Not that they were a *couple* per se, but she was curious as to what they saw or thought seeing them together.

Surprised when Laz reached for her hand, Journey allowed him to lead her around one of the tables and across the dance floor. That's when she noticed Hamilton. He and the woman standing next to him, who Journey assumed was Dakota, were talking to an older couple seated at one of the tables. Hamilton glanced their way and smiled. After excusing themselves, they walked toward her and Laz hand in hand. Dressed in all white, they were a cute pair, but more importantly, they looked happy.

"What's up, lovebirds?" Laz said when the couple got closer. He shook Hamilton's hand and accepted a hug from Dakota before turning back to Journey. "I want you guys to meet someone."

"We've met," Hamilton said, extending his hand. "Good seeing you again, Attorney Ramsey."

"You too, but please, call me Journey."

"Will do, Journey, and this is my wife, Dakota."

"It's a pleasure to meet you," Journey said. Dakota, who was even more stunning up close, looked nothing like Journey had envisioned a stunt woman to look like. She was very feminine and more petite than expected, especially standing next to her hunky husband. "Laz and Dominic speak very highly of you."

Dakota laughed. "Oh, so you've met my little sunshine. He is a talker. Hopefully Dom didn't talk your ear off on the ride here."

"He was fine."

"Dad!" Dominic's voice carried around the room, causing them all to turn in his direction as he dashed across the dance floor toward them.

"Ah, speak of the devil," Hamilton cracked.

"Hey, Dee!" Dominic lunged at her, seeming to soak up the hug she gave him.

"Hey, kid. How was the sleepover?" she asked, placing a kiss on top of his curly hair.

"It was fun." Dominic gave his father a quick hug before returning to Dakota to tell her more about the sleepover. And then he leaned closer to her. "Did you know Uncle Laz had a black girlfriend?"

"Dom!" Hamilton and Laz said at the same time.

Journey burst out laughing, her hand going to her mouth when several people glanced in their direction, but she laughed even harder at the shocked expression of the other three adults.

"I'm going to kill this kid," Laz said under his breath and lunged at Dominic. "What did I tell you in the car?"

"You said she's your *friend*, but I know she's your girlfriend," Dominic said proudly, eyes wide with a huge grin on his face.

"Come here!" Laz growled good-naturedly and Dominic took off running, his laughter traveling behind him as Laz ran after him.

"I don't know what we're going to do with that kid. Sorry about that, Journey," Hamilton said. "He really does have home training, despite the way it seems."

"No harm done. I think he's adorable."

Dakota laughed. "That he is, but that mouth. Girrrl…" She shook her head and looped her arm through Journey's. "Come with me. You and Laz will be sitting at our table and I promise to put Dom somewhere on the other side of the room."

Sharing a laugh, they headed to their seats.

Journey had a feeling she and Dakota were going to get along great.

Chapter Twelve

Laz shook out of his suit jacket and wrapped it around Journey's shoulders. "Better?" he asked. They'd been strolling through the hotel's garden for the last few minutes when he noticed her shiver, then run her hands up and down her arms.

"Much. Thank you. Do you mind if I put it all the way on?"

"No, not at all. Go for it."

Laz waited as she slipped on the jacket and rolled the sleeves up to her wrists. He hated that she was covering up her sexy dress, but he had to admit, he liked seeing her in his clothes.

"Okay, I'm ready."

"Let's head this way. Sounds like there's a water fountain nearby."

"Thanks for inviting me to the reception. Everyone seems so nice and dinner was absolutely delicious. I take it you and Hamilton have known each other a while. His family treats you like one of their own."

Laz smiled and reached for Journey's hand to help her down the concrete stairs. "Yeah, and I consider them my family. Ham and I have known each other since our freshman year of college, and when my parents died a few months apart, the Crosbys stepped in and filled that void. But I felt like one of them before that."

"Oh, yeah?"

Laz nodded. "Ham and I shared a dorm room and one day his mom stopped by with dinner. I fell in love with her the first time I tasted her fried chicken and collard greens."

Journey threw her head back and laughed. "So she hooked you on soul food, huh?"

"She hooked me on food, period. Mind you, my family is Greek. I was used to eating big meals with all my relatives filling a two-bedroom house. But Mrs. Irene—Hamilton's mom—is hands-down the world's greatest cook, and she always cooks a ton of food."

"I guess with three boys...actually four, including you, she probably had to, and it sounds like she still cooks like that. I heard her talking about what she was preparing for dinner tomorrow after church."

Warmth filled Laz's heart as he thought about how supportive the family had been of him. They might not be blood related, but there was nothing he wouldn't do for any of them. He was closer to them than to any of his family.

Laz and Journey stopped near a chest-high brick wall and looked out at the water fountain. Journey looped her arm through his and leaned against his shoulder as if it was the most natural thing to do.

"It's so peaceful out here," she said. The floral scent of her perfume drifted up to his nose, and Laz breathed in deep, embracing the calm that suddenly surrounded him.

"I agree. It's a perfect night."

He didn't usually go on dates and he definitely didn't introduce women to his family, but tonight he'd had more fun than he'd had in a while. Journey was good company. Not only was she easy to talk to, but she had a great sense of humor and seemed like a different person outside of the confines of their jobs. And all night he'd found every excuse to touch her, or pull her against his body like he had when they were dancing, but now he wanted to taste her sweet lips again. Kissing her the other day had only made him long to kiss her over and over again.

Laz mentally shook the thought free. This wasn't a date-date. They were out as friends and he didn't want to do anything that might make her uncomfortable or anything to ruin the night. Sure, they'd flirted throughout the evening, but he had no intention of taking it past that.

"Do you have any siblings?" Journey asked.

"I have an older brother and a sister-in-law who live in Boston."

"Do you guys see each other often?"

Laz shrugged. "Maybe about two or three times a year. Every time we talk, we say we need to get together more often, but you know how it is. Time gets away from you and before you know it, six months has passed."

"Yeah, I know. I heard the older you get, the faster time goes."

"Well, I must be at that point because most of my days are a blur." He chuckled.

Lately, he'd been thinking about the direction of his life, realizing that it was half over, and what had he accomplished? Risking his life on a daily basis to put bad guys away was no longer enough for him; he just wasn't sure what he wanted. Or what he wanted to do with the rest of his life.

"What about you? Besides Geneva, any more siblings?"

"Nah, it's just us and our parents. My dad always said that having Geneva was like having three additional kids, which was why they stopped after her."

Laz laughed, remembering the first time he'd met Geneva at a holiday event she had attended with Journey a year or two ago. She was two years younger than Journey and upon meeting her, he knew the sister was a handful.

Journey told him about her parents who lived a couple of hours away near the border where Georgia connected with Florida. Her mother, an attorney, had her own law firm while her father used to be a detective before he retired.

All the years of knowing her, Laz had no idea her father had been in law enforcement. He wondered what other surprises he didn't know about her.

"How is it that you don't work at your mother's firm?"

She shook her head smiling. "Are you kidding me? We would drive each other nuts if we had to work together. My mom is cool and all, and she's an excellent attorney with an impressive win record. But she's not the easiest person to get along with and could probably win an award for being the most argumentative person to ever live."

"I guess you guys have that in common." Laughing, Laz leaned back to avoid her swatting at him, and then grabbed her wrists. "Hey! Don't get mad at me for speaking the truth. Some days I feel like you live to argue with me."

"That's because you make it so easy. You're always messing up my cases or doing things to piss me off."

Still holding her arms, Laz pulled her closer. Close enough to kiss.

He stared down at her tempting mouth, fighting the desire to cover her lips with his. "Just so you know, I don't intentionally mess up your cases, but I have to be honest. Pissing you off is a serious turn-on."

"Really?" She eased out of his grasp and wrapped her arms around his neck. It wasn't until her hands went to the back of his head and her fingers sifted through his air that his self-control started slipping. "You must be turned on a lot then, because you piss me off all the time."

Laz laughed and slid his arm around her tiny waist and held her against his body. The way his shaft was pushing against his zipper, no doubt she felt just how turned on he was at the moment.

Without waiting for an invitation or asking permission, Laz lowered his head and covered her mouth with his. It was like divine ecstasy whenever he kissed her. Every part of his body came alive when he slipped his tongue between her lips, drinking in her sweetness. Had he known years ago that they would have this type of connection, he would have kissed her long before now.

"If we don't stop now, I won't be able to stop."

"Maybe I don't want you to stop." Journey flirted, her hands smoothing a slow path up his chest, and didn't stop until her hands were cupping his face. They stood that way for the longest as she searched his eyes. What she was looking for, he didn't know, but her touch sent a blast of heat shooting through his body.

Stay strong. We can't do this.

When he didn't say anything, she dropped her hands and smiled up at him. "I get why, and I appreciate you trying to be a gentleman here, but…"

"But it's frustrating as hell," he growled before they both laughed at the situation. "Come on. Let's keep moving before we do something we regret."

If he was honest with himself, Laz knew he wouldn't regret burying himself deep inside of her…at least not right away. But he had a feeling there was going to come a day when neither of them would be able to resist the sexual tension that was growing stronger every minute. It was only a matter of time.

I just hope there won't be any regrets.

Chapter Thirteen

Journey couldn't leave work fast enough. Seemed anything that could've gone wrong did, from breaking a heel on her favorite pair of pumps to having one of her witnesses change her mind about testifying.

The shoe issue was an easy fix since she always kept an extra pair at the office. The witness situation—not so much. She'd been prepping the witness for weeks and to get the call from her that she'd changed her mind, left Journey scrambling for a backup plan. Basically, it had been a hellish week and she was looking forward to joining her sister Geneva for happy hour.

Journey walked out of the building and a blast of heat smacked her in the face. It had to be at least a hundred degrees, even in the shade. *I hate Georgia summers*, she thought as she slipped out of her suit jacket and draped it across her arm. There were only so many articles of clothing she could take off without getting arrested for indecent exposure.

Hoping she didn't have to wait long for her ride, she stretched her neck to glance down the street. Geneva was always running late, but no sooner than the thought filled her mind she spotted her sister's car pull into the no-parking zone.

"Ah, yes. It's officially the weekend," Journey said to

herself, ready to have some fun.

She headed toward the car but stopped abruptly when a tall man in dark shades and a shadow of a beard stopped in front of her.

"You!" he growled in a low, menacing voice. "I know you were behind this."

Her heart lurched in her chest. Assuming he was drunk or high on something, she stepped to the side with intentions of going around him, but he blocked her path. There was something familiar about the guy. She just...

He whipped off his dark glasses and she gasped.

"Gabe! Oh, my God. What happened to you? Who did this?" She set her bag down on the concrete and reached for him, but he swatted her hand away.

"Don't act like you didn't know. Having someone beat me up, Journey? Really?"

"Whoa, whoa, wait a minute," she said, shocked by his allegation.

He pointed at his bruises. "I don't know how, but I'm going to prove that you were behind this."

She took in his swollen face with dark, painful looking circles below his eyes, a bandage across his nose, and puffy lips. His arm was in a sling, though he wasn't in a cast.

She didn't like Gabe, but she wouldn't wish this type of beating on anyone.

"Gabe, I have no idea what you're talking about, but—"

"Save it. You just better watch yourself." He slipped on his sunglasses, despite the setting of the sun and hurried down the street, leaving Journey gawking after him.

Was that a threat?

"Come on, Journey, before I get a ticket!" Geneva yelled through the open window.

Journey hurried toward her sister's vehicle with yet another topic of conversation for them to discuss over drinks.

"I can't believe you think the cutie-pie detective had something to do with Gabe's beatdown," Geneva whispered when they arrived at one of their favorite bar and grills, snagging the last table in the bar area.

"I said I hope he didn't have anything to do with Gabe's situation." Journey didn't want to believe Laz would stoop to that level, but she had a nagging feeling he probably knew something about it.

"I knew Laz had a little thug in him when you introduced me to him last year at that fundraiser." Geneva laughed, and Journey couldn't help but smile. At the time, Geneva had tried flirting with Laz, not knowing that Journey had a serious crush on him.

To Laz's credit, he'd been kind to her sister, but his interest and attention had been solely on Journey. If she had to pinpoint when their relationship had shifted, she could credit it to that evening.

After the server took their drink and appetizer order, Geneva continued.

"You know, I always thought the prosecutor was a little creepy. Remember that Christmas party? He found every excuse to get close to you and then he acted as if he'd been hypnotized by your breasts."

Journey laughed. "Okay, you're right. That was creepy, but he's harmless... At least that's what I used to think. Now, I'm not so sure."

That party had been four years ago and she'd made it clear to Gabe that night she wasn't interested. But lately, something with him had changed and she wondered if his behavior was really about her or if there was something else going on in his life.

"I might have to get the cops involved and let the DA know what's been going on since Gabe threatened me. I don't want to, but he's giving me no other choice."

"Well, from what you told me about that encounter at the courthouse, Gabe is lucky I didn't hunt him down myself and beat his ass. And if Laz wasn't behind the whooping, Gabe must've rubbed someone the wrong way if his face was as bad as you claim."

As the server placed their drinks and potato skins on the table, Journey's thoughts stayed on the Laz and Gabe situation. No way would Laz take that type of risk with the mess that was already going on with him.

Then again, she knew him well enough to know not to put anything past him. He did whatever the heck he wanted to do. Consequences be damned.

"And speaking of Laz, what's going on with you two? Have you had any more kissing sessions since the wedding reception?" Geneva grinned and wiggled her eyebrows. "Or have you guys finally gone to third base? You didn't accidently fall on his dick and not tell me, did you?"

Journey rolled her eyes trying not to laugh; knowing if she did, it would only encourage her sister to continue. Geneva had a way with words and there was nothing off-limits.

"Don't make me regret telling you about the lapse in judgment in my office, and no, nothing's happened between us. I haven't seen or heard from Laz in a week."

"You sound disappointed. Hell, I'd be disappointed if I wanted to screw his brains out and he was nowhere to be found. Sooo, *are* you disappointed? Are you finally ready to get your head out of your ass and let that man show you all that he can do with his tongue?"

"Dang, Geneva! Do Mom and Dad know you talk like that?"

Her sister shrugged and twisted the thin straw around in her drink. "Hey, I just don't understand the problem. The man is absolutely gorgeous. You two have been skirting around each other for years. He likes you. You're crazy about him. Just g'on and fuck and get it over with."

Journey shook her head. "We can't. Well, we could but—"

"Don't tell me it's because he's white."

"Of course not! Laz is a nice guy, and even before we attended the reception, I had gone out with white men before. It's just that..." She kept telling herself that she

90

wanted to maintain a professional relationship with him.

"You know what, sis? I get that you walk this straight and narrow road that you've created for yourself, but life is short. If you want the man, go for it. Use all that." She waved her hands up and down at Journey. "Besides, what if you never act on the attraction between you two? You'll miss out and always wonder what it would have been like to sit on his face and let him eat yo—"

"Stop!" Journey burst out laughing, knowing her sister would have kept going and probably would've gotten more graphic. "What is wrong with you tonight?"

"I'm horny as hell. I honestly don't know how you've gone without for all of these months. Thank God Evan is getting back tonight," she said of her boyfriend of six months. "I've already worn out Dildo Evan and..."

Journey laughed through the rest of her sister's lewd monologue. After the week she'd had, this was exactly what she needed. She hadn't laughed this hard in a long time, probably not since the last time she and her sister got together.

As Geneva explained all that she planned to do to the real Evan when she saw him, Journey's mind drifted to Laz and all that she wouldn't mind doing with him. As promised, he had been the perfect gentleman when they attended the reception. But now she was tired of depriving herself, and what better time than tonight to go after what she wanted?

*

Journey stared out the window as the town car she was riding in the back of traveled through the streets of Atlanta, heading to Laz's place. What seemed like a good idea hours ago was starting to feel like one of the dumbest things she'd done in a while as doubt plagued her mind.

How had she let Geneva talk her into going to see him?

What if he wasn't home? What if he didn't open the door? Or worse, what if he opened the door and didn't let her in?

Journey shook her head. He would never slam the door

in her face. He might give her a hard time about showing up out of the blue, but he'd at least let her in. She wasn't a spontaneous person, and hadn't put a plan fully in place when she and her sister parted ways. All Journey knew was that she didn't want to spend another night alone.

It didn't matter that he was everything fathers warned their daughters about when it came to men. There was an invisible thread that connected her and Laz. A thread she wanted to pull tighter to bring them closer.

Glancing at the bag of food sitting next to her, she knew it would at least get her in the door, assuming he was home. And Gabe's bruised face would give them something to talk about, then she'd leave.

Who are you kidding? You're not gonna want to leave.

Journey rested her head against the leather seat. She wanted Laz more than she wanted anything at the moment. Since neither of them were looking for a serious relationship, it could be the perfect setup. They could act on the scorching attraction between them, without getting emotions involved.

Journey glanced out the window as the car turned into Laz's neighborhood. He lived near Underground Atlanta, and the number of homeless people hanging around stood out like black on a white canvas. Cops didn't make much considering they put their lives on the line daily, but she had a feeling Laz lived in the area to stay close to the action.

Even after the car stopped in front of his building, Journey remained in the back seat. It was still super-hot outside. Yet, people lingered in front of the building laughing, talking loud and smoking. Unease swept through her when she realized she'd have to walk through a group of men near the entrance appearing to be in a heated discussion.

Okay, let's do this.

"Thank you," Journey said to the Uber driver and gathered the bag of food and her purse before climbing out. She held her bags close to her body as she moved quickly to the door, her heels clicking against the concrete.

"You lost?" A kid in his early twenties, with two front

silver teeth blocked her path. The liquor and another smell she couldn't identify on his breath made her eyes water. Journey didn't need this right now. She was already nervous about being there.

"Man, leave her alone," one of the kids he'd been hanging with said before turning back to the small group of guys, but Mr. Silver Tooth didn't move.

Seeing that ignoring him wouldn't work, Journey said, "Thanks, but I know where I'm going." She tried stepping around him, but he blocked her path and grabbed at the sleeve of her shirt.

She yanked her arm back, anger simmering behind her calm. "Touch me again and be prepared to lose that hand," she said in her deadliest voice.

After being attacked years ago, she had taken a self-defense course. Outside of her encounter with Gabe, she hadn't had to use what she'd learned. But she remembered some of the most important body parts to inflict pain. Genitals, eyes, kneecap, and Adam's apple, to name a few. She just hoped she wouldn't have to test her memory.

A shrewd smile spread across his mouth. "I see you have jokes. You think your bony ass can take me?"

"Maybe. If I can't, I'm sure I could get Laz down here to handle you."

The smile immediately dropped from the kid's face and he lifted his hands in surrender. "We're good. Don't need no trouble from the white shadow." He went back to his group, who were now laughing at him.

Journey hadn't known for sure he would know Laz's name, but apparently, he did. No surprise there. There weren't too many people who didn't know of him. Most thought him a nice guy, while the rest thought he was a heartbeat away from crazy.

White shadow?

Journey didn't stick around to question the nickname. She hurried into the building, sidestepping a couple of kids playing cards on the steps, and ignored the loud rap music

93

streaming from one of the apartments. The stench of alcohol mixed with trash was almost too much, but she kept moving.

It wasn't until she arrived on the third-floor landing that she slowed down to catch her breath. Her usual workout was no match for running up the stairs in high heels and a combination of unease and adrenaline pumping through her body. The drinks she'd had earlier probably weren't helping either.

One more flight.

Journey moved the handles of her bags to her other hand, but when she placed her foot on the first step, it slipped.

Crap. She stumbled.

A piercing pain shot through her hand when she tried stopping her fall, and she cried out when the side of her head connected with the metal railing.

Shit.

Staggering, she dropped down on one of the steps waiting for a wave of dizziness to pass.

"Okay girl, get it together," she mumbled to herself as the throb in her head grew. The loud music and the combination of smells only irritated her more while she attempted to regroup.

"I hate when drunk people block the damn steps," a young woman with thick braids down to her butt murmured as she stomped past Journey.

Journey ignored her as she continued holding the side of her head, ensuring the dizziness had passed. It wasn't until she lowered her hand that she noticed blood on her fingers.

So much for spontaneity. The idea to stop by unannounced was getting worse by the minute.

Chapter Fourteen

Laz jerked awake and snatched his gun from the bedside table.

With a finger on the trigger and his outstretched arm moving left then right, his pulse pounded in his ears. He glanced around his darkened space trying to determine what had awakened him.

That's when he heard a knock coming from the living room.

He set the gun down and dropped his head back onto the pillow. Sleep fogged his mind. Seconds ticked by before he lifted his arm and glanced at his watch.

Eight-thirty.

He'd only been asleep a couple of hours. After working a double, he had dragged his exhausted body home and had fallen face-first into bed. He didn't remember anything after that.

Laz's eyes drifted closed. All he needed was a couple of more hours of sleep and he'd be...

Another knock, this time louder, had him sitting up and placing his feet on the floor.

"This shit better be important." He slid into the pair of jeans he'd had at the foot of the bed and didn't bother with a shirt or shoes. With remnants of sleep still clogging his brain, he stuck the pistol into the back of his waistband and stumbled out of the bedroom.

Living in one of Atlanta's toughest neighborhoods, people didn't just stop by.

Laz staggered through the short dark hallway and bumped into the leg of a table when he made it to the living room. "Damn it," he growled, pain shooting through his big toe. Getting madder by the minute at the insistent knocking, he flipped on the living room light.

"What the hell is…" His words lodged in his throat after he swung open the door.

Journey.

Shock immediately turned to concern when a trickle of blood dripped down the side of her face and onto her white shirt.

His heart slammed against his ribcage and anxiety gripped his body. All types of scenarios raced through his mind at once. There was no one behind her, but he couldn't see to her left or her right. All Laz saw was uncertainty in her eyes as she stared at his chest.

On instinct, he eased the gun from the back of his waistband and brought it to his side as he extended his other hand to her. Journey grabbed hold immediately and he tugged her to him, not missing the way she shivered against his body.

What the hell was going on?

He lifted his gun at the ready and glanced into the hall, looking left, then right.

Nothing.

Heart practically beating out of his chest, he stepped back and closed the apartment door with his foot.

"Journey, what's going on?" He did a quick scan down her body. Besides a little shaken, she looked okay except for the cut on the side of her head. But the thought of someone hurting her had his blood boiling.

Eyes wide with her attention on his gun, she still hadn't spoken.

"What happened?" he asked with more calm than he felt,

not wanting to freak her out even more. He set his gun down on the coffee table and took the bags from her hand, placing them on the sofa. With his heart still racing faster than normal, he pulled her into his arms, growing more concerned by her silence.

"If Hall did this, he's a dead man." Laz held her tight, hyperaware of her soft hands on his back. He had received confirmation that Hall had been taken care of. But if that asshole had somehow retaliated by going after Journey, there would be nowhere he could hide that Laz wouldn't find him.

Feeling a sticky liquid drip onto his bare chest, Laz pulled back and looked at the cut. Though small, it seemed to be bleeding more.

"Babe, ya gotta talk to me. I need to know what happened." He grabbed hold of her hand and pulled her to the bathroom. He quickly removed the first-aid kit from the cabinet beneath the sink and set it on the counter. The room was barely big enough for one person. Being in there with her made it a little too cozy for comfort.

"I fell."

Laz's hand stilled on the first-aid cream, and he narrowed his eyes.

"You fell?" he repeated, disbelief dripping from his words. If he had a dollar for every time a domestic violence victim told him that, he'd be rich. Journey wasn't seeing anyone, so he didn't know what to think.

He took a closer look at the cut on the side of her head trying to figure out what type of weapon might've been used. Touching it, he cursed himself for making her flinch. It didn't look deep, but he wouldn't know for sure until he cleaned around it.

"Why don't you tell me what really happened."

"I was coming up the stairs and somehow I missed a step. Then I hit my head on the railing." She went to touch her head, but stopped and stared at the blood on her hand.

"Let's get you cleaned up,"

After she washed her hands, Laz needed her up higher in

order to get a better look at the cut and had her to sit on the counter. All the while he cleaned her wound and patched her up, questions ran rampant through his mind.

"Ow, Laz," Journey whimpered, wincing when he put a Band-Aid on her cut.

"Sorry."

Once he was finished, he placed his hands on the counter on either side of her. Bending down slightly, he brought them face to face.

God, she looks so small and vulnerable. He wanted to wrap his arms around her and never let go.

Unable to help himself, he brushed his lips across hers.

"Let me get this right. You fell on the stairs," he said, still having a hard time believing that's what really happened. But he had to admit that he was glad she came to him.

Journey cut her eyes at him. "Why do I have a feeling you don't believe me?"

Laz said nothing. He didn't want to argue. He hoped that was all that happened and that she wasn't attacked and keeping it from him.

"So what was with the panicked look when I opened the door? Are you sure yo—"

"Laz, I'm telling you the truth. It's hard to admit because I feel like a big doofus, but I really did fall on the stairs. Nothing else. I promise."

He stood and folded his arms across his chest as she continued.

"If I looked panicked, it was probably because of the way you came to the door. You had a gun. Your hair was sticking up all over the place and...and..." her hands flew around as she spoke, "...you're practically naked...looking all sexy and shit. Hell, you caught me off guard!"

After a few seconds, he fell out laughing and then laughed harder at the serious expression on her face. "Have you been drinking?"

Her brows dipped into a frown. "I might've had a couple of drinks after work, but I'm not drunk!" she snapped.

He grinned, loving her fire. It was that spitfire side of her that made him enjoy their verbal sparrings when discussing a case.

His gaze went from her fiery eyes to her luscious mouth. Against his better judgment, he lowered his head and nipped and teased her top lip, and then her bottom one before sliding his tongue into her sweet mouth.

Memories of their tongue aerobics from the week before had burned a permanent spot in his mind. Over and over he'd told himself *never again*. Never would he lose control with her the way he had that day in her office.

At the reception, he'd been able to exercise some self-control, but right now...he couldn't help himself. He needed the feel of her mouth against his. In the last twenty minutes, his heart rate had jockeyed up and down, thanks to her, and this...this calmed his nerves.

When Laz finally released her mouth, he thought about something she'd said. "You think I'm sexy, huh?"

She rolled her eyes. "You know good and damn well you're sexy."

He laughed again. "When did you start cursing so much?"

"I've been hanging out with my sister. She curses almost as much as you do. I guess in that short amount of time together she rubbed off on me."

Laz remembered Geneva. Now that was a woman who scared the hell out of him. She was movie-star beautiful with a slamming body to match, but her boldness and the way she spoke her mind would make any man run for cover.

Laz stood to his full height and twisted a bit to work the kinks out of his shoulders and back. "Why don't you take that top shirt off so we can get the bloodstains out before they dry."

He helped Journey off the counter and she looked down at the spots on her white shirt. "Is this you trying to get me naked?"

Now Laz was the one caught off guard. With her

question and the way she was looking at him through lowered lashes, he wasn't sure if she was serious or just messing with him.

He didn't bother responding. Yes, he wanted her naked, but wanting and acting on it were two very different things.

Journey removed the bloodstained top, leaving her wearing a lace spaghetti-strap camisole. There were a few areas where the blood had soaked through, but not as much as the other shirt.

Aw, hell. No bra.

His dick twitched. The sight of her nipples standing at attention against the lace called out to him, begging him to suck on them. With the thinness of the material, he could easily make out the dark areolas of her glorious breasts. And the view had the blood in his brain shooting south, making him as hard as granite.

Journey looked at him innocently. "I guess I'll have to take this one off, too."

"Journey, don't fuck with me," he said under his breath and went across the hall to his bedroom, his dick painfully hard. He hadn't had sex in months and the slightest temptation was bound to push him to do something he had no intention of doing.

Rambling through his dresser drawer, he had to find the biggest, thickest T-shirt he owned. There was no way in hell he could be around her half-dressed body and not take her to bed.

*

Journey burst out laughing at how fast Laz ran from the bathroom. So far the evening hadn't gone the way it had played out in her head earlier. She'd had every intention of them talking over hamburgers about Gabe, and then she'd planned to seduce Laz.

Now the burgers were probably cold and Laz was acting skittish. She had no idea how she was going to get him to treat her like any other woman, and not think about their professional relationship.

"What are you afraid of, Laz?" Journey asked from the bedroom doorway.

He stopped rummaging through his collection of T-shirts and glanced over his shoulder. A very muscular, tanned shoulder that went well with the rest of his well-built upper body. A body that had no fat anywhere and called to her.

"Right now I'm afraid of you," he muttered.

She laughed again at the seriousness of his tone. "You don't have to fear me. I won't bite, unless you want me to."

He grunted but didn't comment and Journey moved farther into the room, taking in his space. The bedroom was nothing like the living room that had dull beige walls with no pictures, and furniture that had seen better days. Instead, the bedroom looked warm and inviting. The king-sized bed with a fabric-covered headboard that went to the ceiling took up most of the space. The walls were a soft blue with artwork strategically placed, as well as curtains and a comforter to bring all the colors together.

"This room is stunning. Why doesn't the rest of the apartment look like this?"

Laz shrugged. "This is the most important room in the place. Where I spend most of my time."

"Oh," she said with more disappointment than intended. Maybe the rumors of him having a different woman every night were true.

"Get your head out of the gutter. I've never brought a woman here," he said as if reading her mind. "The last thing I need is some clingy-ass woman showing up on my doorstep at all times of the night. Here, put this on and don't even think about taking that lacy…thing off." He shoved the navy-blue Atlanta Braves T-shirt into her hands and left her in the room.

Journey stood stunned, holding the T-shirt. "Are you saying that I'm clingy?" she asked kicking off her heels and removing the lace top before slipping into his shirt, ignoring how it went almost to her knees. While she was at it, she slipped out of her pants and tossed them in a nearby chair.

Going out there in only his shirt and her panties would be a bold move, but she was on a mission.

Journey backtracked to the living room. "So, are you?"

"Am I…" He stopped, his gaze taking in her attire, but he didn't comment, only cleared his throat. "Am I what?"

"Are you saying that I'm clingy?" She noticed at some point he had slipped into a T-shirt, to her disappointment. She would much rather see him shirtless.

"Journey, I'm not talking about you." He opened the bag of food that was on the sofa and inhaled. "Good, hamburgers and fries. I'm starving. Let's eat."

Laz quickly warmed their food in the microwave, moving around with the efficiency of a man who spent time in the kitchen. When he snatched a beer and a bottle of water out of the refrigerator, he grumbled something under his breath as if he was mad at the world.

"Is that sexual frustration you're taking out on the food and those poor defenseless bottles?" she taunted, ignoring his low growl that floated from the kitchen.

Standing near the small dinette table gave her a view into the tiny kitchen. She didn't know what she expected, but she was a little surprised to see everything so neat and clean. Now she knew why he called her a slob.

"Have a seat so we can eat." He slammed the water bottle down in front of her and took a long drag from his beer.

Journey smirked behind her hand, enjoying how rattled he was. "How do you know I didn't want a beer?"

"I have a feeling you've had enough to drink tonight." He took a huge bite of his hamburger. "What's going on? Why are you here?"

"Would you believe I was in the neighborhood?"

"No. Try again."

"I thought you might be hungry, so I brought dinner."

A slow smile spread across Laz's mouth. "Is that right? You know, you're cute when you're trying to play all innocent. Tell me what really brought you to my neighborhood."

They ate in silence until she said, "I ran into Gabe after work today."

Laz tensed. His hazel-green eyes studied her, growing darker the longer he looked at her. "Did he—"

"He didn't touch me, but it seemed someone had definitely put their hands on him."

"Oh yeah?"

"Yeah, and they messed him up pretty bad. You wouldn't happen to know anything about that, would you?"

"I have no idea what you're talking about," he said with a straight face. There was no remorse in his tone and if she didn't know better, she would believe him. But she knew better.

"I think he threatened me."

Laz's gaze snapped to her. "What? What did he say?"

"He told me he knows I had something to do with the beatdown. As if I know people who do stuff like that." Having second thoughts about whether or not to tell him the rest, Journey toyed with her napkin.

"What else did he say?"

She looked into Laz's eyes and after a long hesitation, said, "He told me that I had better watch myself."

"Oh, hell no!" Laz lunged from his seat and backed away from the table. He ran both hands through his tousled hair before he turned back to her. "Journey, if he ever comes near you again, you have to tell me."

"When I arrived here bleeding, you said that if Hall did this, he's a dead man. Did you mean that?"

"*Every* word."

"Laz." Journey said his name, but didn't know how to respond to the conviction in his admission. Knowing he thought like this, there was no way she'd tell him anything else that happened between her and Gabe.

They ate the rest of their meal in silence, each in their own thoughts.

Journey should've felt flattered that he cared that much

to fight her battles, but on the other hand, his words scared her. She believed he would actually hurt Gabe if he stepped out of line, and she would never forgive herself if Laz ended up in jail because of her.

"We're going to have to do something about Gabe," Laz finally spoke.

No way was Journey asking what that something was. "I'm going to move forward in filing a formal complaint against him, and if necessary, I'll get a restraining order. And that's all *we're* going to do right now."

Laz rubbed the back of his neck and Journey could tell he wasn't satisfied with her response. He stood and gathered their trash, tossing the wrappers in the garbage before returning to his seat.

"Tell me, counselor. *Do* you know people who could have given Gabe that beatdown? Should I be worried that you'll send someone after me one day?"

The right corner of her lips inched up. "If I knew someone like that, he probably would've already paid you a visit the first time you screwed up one of my cases."

Laz threw his head back and laughed, loosening some of the tension in the room. "I don't know why you always accuse me of screwing up your cases, woman. My job is to get these chumps off the street. It's your job to make sure they stay off." He shrugged. "I can't help it if you drop the ball sometimes."

"Yeah, whatever."

Laz finished off his beer. "Thanks for dinner. It was right on time. Do you want something else to drink?"

"Do you have something stronger than water?"

Laz flashed that grin that she loved so much. "Yeah, but like I said earlier, I think you've had enough alcohol."

"I told you. I'm not drunk."

"Maybe, but your actions and words tonight say otherwise." He looked her up and down, lingering on her bare legs. "And I have a feeling that your run-in with Gabe isn't your only reason for stopping by. Are you ready to tell me the real reason for this visit?"

She toyed with the tail of the oversized T-shirt she was wearing, debating on whether to go through with her original plan.

It's now or never.

She stood from her seat and straddled his lap.

The surprised expression on his face—priceless.

"I wanted to see you. All of you."

Chapter Fifteen

Ah hell.

Laz didn't know what he'd expected her to say, but it wasn't that. And where the heck were her clothes? With her sitting on his lap, grinding against him, it was clear what she wanted. What they both wanted.

And therein lay the problem.

"I'm tired of ignoring this…this thing between us. I want you. I want to feel you buried balls-deep inside of me. And don't worry, I'm not looking for a commitment. Actually, I don't do commitments."

Laz leaned back and grabbed her chin to look into her eyes. "Are you sure you're not drunk?"

She sighed dramatically and swatted his hand away. "I'm not drunk, Laz! Horny, but not drunk."

If they crossed that invisible line that they'd drawn, the line that kept them from ripping each other's clothes off way before now, there would be no turning back.

"What do you mean you don't do commitments?"

"I don't do commitments mainly because men start treating you different once you agree to *go steady*." She laughed. "Exciting dates eventually turn into boring nights watching TV or silent, boring dinners together. My parents have been married for over forty years and though I know they love each other, their lives seem so…so boring."

"I see."

"I'm not asking for long-term, Laz. I'm not asking for marriage. But I am interested in a friends-with-benefits relationship. You and I want the same thing."

"You think that I'd be satisfied with just fucking you?" He moved her firmly onto his erection and held her steady, wanting her to feel how much he wanted her. He nipped at her scented neck. And then he sucked. Already marking his territory. If she was ready, the way she claimed, then who was he to deny her? But he needed to make something clear.

"Mmm, Laz," she purred and looped her arms around his neck and dropped her head back, giving him better access as she rocked on top of him. He only had so much control; a little bit more and his dick was going to punch a hole through his pants. But he needed an answer.

"You didn't answer me, Journey."

"A little less talk and a little more action, detective."

It was crazy. He had this fine-ass woman basically begging for him, ready to let him do whatever he wanted with her. Yet, he couldn't move forward until they had an understanding. He grabbed hold of her arms and pulled them from around his neck.

"I want a commitment."

She froze. If he was honest, his words shocked him, too. Sure, he'd had his share of one-night stands, and his go-to women when he needed release, but this was the first time since Gwenn that he wanted more. He wanted Journey. He had denied himself long enough and wanted her in every way a man could want a woman.

"You can't be serious."

"I'm dead serious. I'm crazy about you, and I'm not looking for a quick lay. Hell, had that been all I wanted from you, we would've had sex years ago."

She chuckled. "Arrogant much?"

"I'm just telling you like it is. I have the utmost respect for you and have kept my distance to make sure that I don't…that I don't taint you with my shit. But like you, I'm tired of denying myself when it comes to you. I kept my distance because I didn't want my reputation to affect your career in any way, nor did I want to mess up our friendship. But now, I want you. All of you."

She bit her bottom lip and studied him. "I don't do commitments, Laz. I like not answering to anyone. I love coming and going as I please. Besides, my job and work schedule aren't conducive to a successful relationship. I've tried before and I can't do it. I don't want marriage. I don't want children."

"Then you don't want me."

Her mouth formed a perfect O. "I didn't say that," she said quickly when he started to lift her off his lap. "Why are you being so difficult?"

He grunted. "*I'm* being difficult because I want you?"

She dropped her head to his chest. "You're really killing my buzz."

"Oh, so you are drunk," he cracked. She laughed, but didn't lift her head. Kissing the side of her hair he said, "All or nothing, Journey. If we do this, you're mine. All mine."

She lifted up, her gaze on his mouth and then his eyes.

"If things don't work out," he shrugged, "then we go our separate ways. What's it going to be? Want to give me a shot? Want to give *us* a shot?"

Instead of answering, she kissed him. Not just a little, sweet, gentle kiss, but a kiss that left no doubt as to her answer. That was all Laz needed to hear…or feel.

He pulled his mouth from her despite her protests and lifted the shirt over her head, tossing it in the chair she'd vacated. He'd been dying to see her naked, her dark skin gleaming under his fluorescent lights.

"Damn you're beautiful."

"Thank you," she said quietly, suddenly looking shy with her brown eyes softening and a timid smile on her lips. Lips he planned to enjoy.

Laz crushed his mouth to hers with a hunger he hadn't

felt since the last time he'd kissed her. Even in his wildest dreams, he hadn't expected her to come to him so ready, willing and open.

Journey held the back of his head firmly as their kiss deepened and she continued grinding her body on top of his. His penis throbbed behind his zipper, begging to be free, but he'd waited too long for her. No way would he rush this. He planned to savor every last inch of her body before the night was over.

Without breaking contact, he nudged her panties aside and slid his thumb over her slit.

"Mmm," he moaned against her mouth. "You're so wet for me."

He felt her smile against his lips before pulling back slightly.

"I've been waiting a long time for..." Her voice hitched and her words trailed off into an erotic moan when he slid a finger into her tightness and then another.

Damn she's hot, Laz thought as he moved his fingers in and out of her. Going deeper, faster and harder, loving the erotic sounds she made with each lengthy stroke. He still found it hard to believe that she was there, in his house, on his lap, and making him harder than granite as she swiveled around his digits. It was all like a dream that he never wanted to wake up from.

He leaned forward and sucked on her long, scented neck when her head lolled back. He accepted the sweet torture of her fingernails clawing his shoulders as she rode his hand faster. With each rotation of her hips, her moves became jerky. Her breathing more labored.

"Laz," she whimpered, grinding harder, holding him tighter.

"I'm right here. Come for me."

With those few words, an orgasm ripped from her, jostling her body like trees swaying through a wind storm. She came hard and fast, screaming his name before collapsing against his chest.

Totally spent, her body trembled with aftershocks, her breaths warm near his ear. Laz kissed the side of her damp head, feeling a possessiveness he couldn't explain. All he knew was, she was his.

He moved slightly. Digging through his back pocket, he was glad he hadn't left his wallet in the bedroom. He pulled out the condom and then dropped the wallet on the floor.

"Baby, I'm going to need you to stand up for a minute."

She shook her head, her hair brushing against his chin. "I—I can't…move."

Laz chuckled. "You're going to have to because I need you out of your panties. I'm not done with you."

"Good to know, but Laz, just give me a min…"

He wiggled enough to get his jeans started over his hips before she moaned in pleasure. Hell, he'd just work around the little strip of garment if he had to. As if reading his mind, she lifted her head, a lazy grin covering her juicy lips.

When she stood, Laz could barely focus on discarding his pants and boxer briefs as she guided the little slip of lace down her long shapely legs. His shaft was standing at attention, throbbing for release as he quickly sheathed himself.

"Come here," he said after reclaiming his seat.

*

Journey knew Laz would look magnificent, but the sight of his thick erection almost made her come before she could feel him inside her. She held onto his hand as he guided her on top of his length, filling her completely.

"Damn, you feel good," he murmured, his large hands gripping her hips as she adjusted to his size.

"Ohhh," she moaned when his mouth covered one of her nipples and he started moving beneath her. With every swirl of his tongue over her hardened peak, her muscles contracted around his shaft as he buried himself deeper inside her.

She savored the way he took his time with each breast, giving them equal amounts of attention and loving on them as if he couldn't get enough of her. Running her fingers through his hair, something she loved doing, Journey held his head close as her impending climax grew near.

Oh yes, this was what she'd been waiting for, pining for when they'd been trying to keep their distance from each other. And being with him like this was so worth the wait.

When she lifted slightly, sliding up and down his penis with long, even strokes, rotating her hips to the rhythm he'd set, Laz pulled his mouth from her body and groaned.

"Aw, yes." His fingers dug into the bottom of her thighs and he lifted her up and down his length as if she weighed nothing. His strength was impressive, but so was the rest of him.

With each move, the wood chair creaked under their weight, but Journey barely noticed. His passionate grunts and powerful thrusts, and the feel of him buried to the hilt dominated her attention, pushing her closer to her release and sending a new wave of pleasure pumping through her body.

"Laz!" she gasped when he hit that sweet spot. She was unable to form any other words, her hands fisting in his hair, holding on tight as he picked up speed, pumping into her.

Harder. Faster.

Until she lost total control.

Her body bucked and bounced on top of him and with another hard thrust, he pushed her over the edge.

Laz growled, murmuring something she couldn't decipher just as his release gripped him. The powerful explosion of his orgasm ripped through him hard enough to rock them both.

They collapsed against each other, their heavy breathing mingling in the quietness of the room.

"Aww, Journey," Laz panted, his head against her shoulder still struggling for air. Neither of them said anything for the longest time as they slowly caught their breaths.

"Are you okay?" Laz gently gripped her face between his hands, his eyes full of concern. "I didn't hurt you, did I?"

She shook her head. "No. I'm better than okay."

Chapter Sixteen

Hours later and bone tired, Journey lay in Laz's bed with her eyes barely opened. She knew they'd be explosive together, but what they'd just shared exceeded her wildest fantasy.

Laz pulled her back on top of him, his penis rigid between her thighs.

"Again? You're insatiable, detective."

"Only with you. Do you have any idea how long I've waited to be with you? Now I can't get enough."

His words reminded her of their conversation in the kitchen. Never in a million years would she have thought him the commitment type. She assumed he was like her, not wanting the complications that often came with committed relationships.

"I'm wondering if we need to get you to the hospital." He turned her head slightly. "That's the second Band-Aid that you've soaked through. There's a small, dull maroon spot coloring the outside of the bandage. I'm starting to wonder if your cut is deeper than I originally thought. Does your head still hurt?"

Journey thought for a moment. To be honest, she hadn't really noticed since he'd kept her busy. "Maybe a little, but I'll be fine."

"Okay, but we should keep an eye on it."

Journey placed a kiss on his bare chest, appreciating his concern. "So what is it about me that... Why me, Laz? Why do you want to be with me when I'm not your usual type?"

He rubbed her back with slow, gentle movements, studying her in that way that always got her feminine juices stirring. "What's my usual type?"

Journey didn't know for sure since she had never seen him with a woman, but she had heard about his type. "Tall, shapely with big breasts, long red hair, and white."

At five-foot eight, Journey was taller than most women, and her size eight could definitely be considered shapely, but that's where the similarities stopped. She wore her hair in a short, cropped style most of the time, and fell somewhere between a B and C bra cup on a good day. And the most notable difference—she was black.

Laz rolled them over onto their sides facing each other, chest to chest, thigh to thigh. One of his long legs draped over hers, holding her firmly in place. "I'm not going to even ask where you got your information from, but don't forget nice legs. I'm definitely a leg man."

Heat rose to her cheeks when he looked at her pointedly. She had caught him on more than one occasion checking out her legs. It was because of his attention that she wore skirts most days.

Journey touched his face, rubbing her hands over the stubble on his cheek, the contrast of their skin color drawing her attention. She had dated outside of her race before, but never anything serious.

"But to answer your question, why not you? You're brilliant, gorgeous, have a great sense of humor, and you can hold your own whenever we disagree on a subject. That's a real turn-on, by the way. As for being black, I don't care about your race. It's you, the person, that I fell for. Not just your looks."

Journey's heart sang at his words. Granted, she had tripped all over herself when they first met because of his intriguing eyes, but she also found him fascinating.

"I was attracted to you immediately, and over the years that I've gotten to know you, my feelings for you have intensified," he continued.

She touched his lower lip, and he opened his mouth and sucked on her fingertip. Butterflies fluttered inside her belly at the sexy move.

"So why me, Journey? You're an amazing woman who turns heads wherever you go. Why consider dating me?"

"I like you and I love the way I feel when I'm near you." She didn't tell him that being near him made her want to take her usual straight and narrow path and add a few twists and turns. She had always been considered a *good girl*, but Laz made her want to throw out caution and live a little.

"Also, though I might not agree with everything you do," she continued, "I love the passion in which you do things. You have this badass vibe and reputation about yourself. Yet, the way you treat me and some of the victims you come in contact with, shows you have heart."

"Sounds like you've given this some thought."

She nodded. "I have. The attraction has been mutual, I just wasn't sure it was a good idea to act on what I felt for you. So, what do we do now?"

Laz pulled her even closer, his large hand cupping one of her butt cheeks. "I have a few ideas."

She laughed, but then moaned when he started kneading her bottom, causing her to rub against his hard shaft as he planted soft kisses along the length of her neck. Considering the ardent surge of yearning pulsing through her body, if he kept it up, they were going to end up going another round despite the soreness between her thighs.

"Though I like the way you think, I was actually wondering where do we go from here. What exactly does it mean to be in a relationship with you?"

Laz pulled back slightly. "Now is a fine time to ask. Shouldn't you have gotten all the facts before moving forward with me? I'm a little surprised, counselor."

"What? I was sitting on your lap when you laid out your conditions. Your huge package between my legs was distracting. I couldn't focus. So I guess you can say I agreed to your terms under duress."

Laz laughed, the hardiness of the tone making her smile. "That's the defense you're planning to use? You weren't under duress when you teased me with your luscious breasts in the bathroom, using them like weapons."

"Ha! Is that why you were running? You felt threatened by my boobs?" She wiggled her upper body, her breasts swinging in his face.

"Don't. I can't handle it when you do that," he groaned and palmed one of them, lowering his mouth over her sensitive nipple. Her body tingled with the contact and her eyes fluttered closed as his tongue licked and swirled around the tip.

"And I—I can't think straight when you do that," she moaned and ran her hands through his hair, pulling slightly. Once she regained some control and had his attention again, she said, "I'm still trying to get an understanding of what it'll be like to date you. How do you feel about PDA?"

He lay on his back and stretched his arms out and yawned before fluffing his pillow. "What's PDA?"

"Public displays of affection."

"You should know me well enough to know that I do whatever the hell I want. If that means kissing you in front of everybody and their mama..." he shrugged, "...I'll do whatever feels right at the moment."

Journey wasn't sure what to say to that. Tony was the only man she'd ever dated for any real length of time and he wasn't into PDA, which was all right with her.

"With that said, though," Laz continued and ran the back of his fingers down her cheek, "Starting today, I'll never do anything, whether you're around me or not, that I think will hinder your job or your reputation."

"Yeah, right. Promises, promises."

"You have my word, Journey. Everything by the book

going forward. No exceptions."

Searching his eyes, his gaze didn't waver. She believed him. Or at least she believed he'd try.

"Okay, detective, I guess we're officially dating."

Journey raised up and covered his mouth with hers, again falling under the spell that he kept putting on her whenever their lips touched.

Laz cupped her face between his large hands. He could be so gentle sometimes, making it hard to remember that he could also be just as dangerous.

"There's something you should probably know," he said.

"Laz, if you tell me that this was all a joke, I'm going to hurt you."

He smiled. "I'm serious about everything we've discussed, and I'm also very protective, Journey. Especially of those who mean anything to me. The shit I see out on these streets on a daily basis might have me being overbearing, but just know that it's coming from a good place. You're important to me and I can't help but want to look out for you."

"Does that mean that you *did* have something to do with Gabe getting beat up?"

"I told you before, I have no idea what you're talking about."

Yeah right.

"Now can we finally get a few hours of sleep before the sun comes up?" He turned off the lamp on his side of the bed without waiting for a response, bathing the room in darkness except for the soft light coming from the hallway.

Journey relaxed in the crook of his arm, her head resting beneath his chin as her fingers drew circles on his chest. She found comfort lying next to him, his hand caressing her hip. Had anyone told her that she'd be spending the night with Lazarus Dimas, she would have laughed in their face. And now look at her. They were official.

Wow. Me and Laz.

She lifted her head slightly, sensing he had dozed off. No

doubt he was tired, but she was too wired to sleep.

"Laz?"

"Hmm," he grunted and started back caressing her hip.

"Does you wanting to be in a relationship have anything to do with Gwenn Andreou?"

Laz stiffened against her and Journey suddenly regretted the question. She couldn't help but be curious about his late girlfriend. The little that she'd found on her was sketchy at best.

"I'm done with answering questions tonight," Laz said quietly and moved her hand from his chest. Sitting up, he placed his feet on the floor and stood. "I'm going to take a shower."

*

Laz stood directly under the rainfall showerhead. The warm water cascading over his body like a soothing balm relieved some of his tension.

Why was it that whenever Gwenn's name was mentioned, it was like reliving that dark time in his life all over again? He had to figure out how to stop shutting down whenever anyone questioned him about her.

It was past time to move on. He had taken out his own type of revenge on the people responsible for her murder, and had spent years in therapy. Yet there was still a part of his heart that hadn't healed.

Because you won't let it heal.

He turned his face up to the water and pushed his wet hair out of his eyes. He shouldn't have walked away from Journey. If he wanted this relationship to work, he had to be willing to open up to her, the way he expected her to do.

Laz wiped some of the water from his face when he heard the bathroom door open and close. Moments later, the shower curtain slid back slightly and Journey stood in the narrow opening, standing before him in all her naked glory. He felt like the luckiest man alive. He would never get tired of looking at her, nude or not.

"I'm sorry," she said, her voice low, and her eyes unsure.

She was such a beautiful contradiction. On one hand, a kick-ass attorney who had put away her share of scumbags, and on the other hand, a soft, vulnerable woman who he had fallen hard for.

Laz extended his hand and pulled her into the shower. "You have nothing to be sorry about."

He turned her away from the shower head, ensuring not to get her hair wet.

"I know you're tired and I shouldn't have intruded in your personal life. I guess I—"

"You're a part of my personal life now. You have every right to ask me anything you want. I'm the one who's sorry. I shouldn't have walked away."

He lifted her chin with the pad of his index finger and kissed her lips. He hadn't let a woman get this close to him, emotionally, since Gwenn. It was time.

"I'll tell you anything you want to know."

"Okay, but since we're in here. We might as well get cleaned up. Or maybe…" Her words trailed off and she wrapped her arms around his neck, capturing his mouth in a wicked kiss.

"Aw, baby," Laz moaned against her mouth, backing her up against the shower wall. Their tongues tangled, exploring the inner recesses of each other's mouths and he didn't know how much he could handle before losing total control. The deep, searing kiss, and the caress of her lips against his made him powerless to resist anything she offered. They had resisted each other for so long, but he had a feeling the getting-acquainted stage of the relationship was going to be a blast.

A sensual charge shot through Laz when her hand slid slowly between their bodies and she gripped his engorged shaft. He groaned. The sound thick with need as she slid her hand languidly up and down, stroking, squeezing, heightening the desire roaring through his veins. When her thumb brushed across the tip of his dick, Laz almost lost it.

Journey gasped when he lifted her. A small squeal of

delight filling the tight space as he cradled her butt in his hands. She held on as her legs went easily around him, and he slid between her slick folds, feeling as if he had finally made it home.

Waves of ecstasy ricocheted through his body as he drove into her hard and fast, her breasts brushing the fine hairs on his chest with every thrust. That sensation only made him go harder, deeper, as he got lost in her sweet heat. She matched him stroke for stroke and when her body tightened around him, Laz knew his release was close.

One last push and she came hard, convulsing in his arms, and a hot tide of passion raged through his body catapulting him over the edge. Weak in the knees, he staggered a bit before lowering her body until her feet touched the floor of the shower.

Man, that was...

Laz rested his forehead against the tile, unable to do much else as he caught his breath. Having sex in the shower hadn't been planned, but sure had been enjoyable, he thought as he held her around the waist. He couldn't remember the last time he had...

"Oh shit."

"If that expletive is about our lack of a condom, I'm on birth control," Journey said, breathing hard near his ear.

Laz relaxed, though he was pissed he'd slipped up.

"That was incredible," she panted. "But, Laz, I don't think I can move."

He chuckled and drummed up what little energy he had left. "I got you, babe."

Holding onto her, he got them cleaned up and ran a towel over their wet bodies, not caring that they weren't completely dry. When they made it to the bed and Journey's head hit the pillow, her soft snores started before he could even get settled. He had never seen anyone fall asleep that fast, but felt a little proud knowing their lovemaking had worn her out.

He pulled the sheet over them and stared down at her

sleeping form, barely able to keep his own eyes open. He didn't know what the future held for them, but he planned to put all of his energies into making their relationship work. He just hoped he didn't screw it up.

Hours later, Laz woke slowly. A sliver of sunlight crept through the spot where the curtains were pulled together. There was no way it could be morning already.

Without moving, he glanced down at the top of Journey's head nestled against his chest. She was sprawled over him, her arm and leg across his body as if she were trying to hold him down.

Feeling as if he had run a marathon—twice—his eyes drifted closed. Thankfully, he had the day off. Journey had zapped him of all energy and if given the opportunity, he could sleep for a week. He must have dozed off because when he reopened his eyes, she was staring up at him.

"Good morning," she mumbled.

"Morning, beautiful." Now this he could get used to. Waking up to her sweet face beat the hell out of waking up alone in bed.

Journey lifted up and started to move off of him, but he stopped her with a hand on her back. "Where you going?"

"Well, I was getting off of you so that you could breathe." She flashed a shy smile. Surely, she wasn't implying that she was heavy.

"I like you laying on top of me, and I love waking up to you."

She smiled and it was as if the whole room lit up. "I like waking up to you, too." She scooted up higher and kissed him. "I'm hungry."

"I guess I should get up and feed you then." Thoughts of the conversation they never had the night before came to mind. "But first we need to talk."

"If this is about Gwenn, I told you last night that you don't have to tell me."

"I want to."

This time when she made a move to climb off of him, he

didn't stop her.

How was he going to share the darkest time of his life with her? Just thinking about the year after Gwenn's murder made him want to shut down. It did help that Journey snuggled next to him, and his arm automatically went around her, needing to have her close.

"My first year as a detective, I cracked a case that the department had been working on for years. There was a big-time drug dealer who had relocated the bulk of his business from Chicago to Atlanta. Like most detectives, I was hungry for a big case. Cocky, and I had something to prove, not just to myself, but to some of the other detectives." Laz exhaled loudly, as the memories flooded to the forefront of his mind. "I was determined to take this drug supplier off the streets, especially since he'd been evading arrest, and I got him. Caught him with his pants down, literally. There were enough drugs in his possession to put him away for life."

Without realizing it, Laz moved his arm from around Journey and pulled away, but with a hand on his torso she looked up at him.

"It's time you stopped running, Laz. Tell me the rest."

He stared at her for a minute, surprised at her words. His coping mechanism had always been to keep moving and avoid questions. But he knew she was right.

Huffing out a breath, he laid his head back on the pillow and stared up at the ceiling, trying to get his thoughts together.

"After this guy was convicted, I went after his whole operation." Laz closed his eyes tightly and pinched the bridge of his nose, trying to hold onto his composure.

"On second thought, if this is too painful, maybe—"

"Long story short, those bastards pumped heroin into Gwenn, but made it look like she had ODed. She didn't do drugs. *Ever*. She had just received her master's in environmental science and... She was curious about everything, always needing to find answers and crazy smart, too." He squeezed Journey, trying to find strength in her being there beside him. "I guess I have a thing for smart women."

Laz tried to return Journey's smile, but anxiety roared through him.

"I found her...dead," he choked out before clearing his throat.

Journey laid her head on his shoulder and wrapped her arm around him. Strangely enough, that simple move brought him a comfort he had never felt when discussing that horrific time in his life. "When I arrived home that night, the back door to our house was standing wide open. I knew then they'd gotten to her."

"Oh my, God, Laz. I'm so sorry. No one should have to—"

"I lost it, Journey. I fuckin' lost my shit." He shook his head, trying to wipe the vision of her body lying lifeless on the floor near the sofa. "I went after the whole fucking organization like a man possessed, starting at the bottom and working my way up until I got to the second-in-command. I had nothing to lose, at least that's how I felt at the time. Journey, I did some things..."

Silence filled the room, narrowing like a noose around his neck, the knot tightening with each passing second. Laz debated on just how much to tell her. He could easily be spending his life behind bars for the shit he did back then, but he'd gotten lucky.

Journey placed a finger on his lips when he started to speak again. "I've heard enough. Thank you for telling me." Her finger was then replaced by her lips in a lingering kiss that brought with it a sense of understanding and no judgment. "I hate you had to go through that, but it explains your low tolerance for drug dealers."

Laz had *no* tolerance for drug dealers. Since that night, he had vowed to clear the city of as many of them as possible. Some days were better than others in accomplishing that goal, whereas other days he just wanted to walk away and never look back.

Indebted

If you're ever looking for a change... Hamilton's words floated inside Laz's head. Maybe it was time for a change.

Time to let go. And time to move on.

Chapter Seventeen

"We're a family. We always have each other's back," Malik Lewis, the founder of Supreme Security, said in front of the group of security specialists. "All of us are accustomed to working as a team and being a part of a brotherhood and sisterhood of protectors. Whether you have a military background or law enforcement experience, the bond you had with your brothers while serving the country or the bond you had with your brothers in blue—that's the same type of connection we have aspired to create here at Supreme."

Laz listened as Malik went on to tell the group more about the company, even though Laz had heard a similar speech from Mason and Hamilton. But Malik, who some referred to as Tree, since he stood at 6'8", impressed Laz with his forward thinking. The former Navy SEAL had started the security agency in Chicago after retiring from the military. The company not only offered personal security, but also residential and corporate security. Since its conception, Supreme had expanded to Atlanta with talks of opening offices in other cities.

"Over the next few weeks, either Mase or Ham will give you more detail about our collaboration with the event planning company," Malik said. "Now, I don't know about you guys, but I have to get the hell out of here. My wife and kids are expecting me back at the hotel in thirty minutes, and with Atlanta's fucked-up traffic, I..." He stopped and shook his head when everyone started laughing.

Laz had heard that the big man had a serious cursing problem that he'd been trying to clean up now that he was married with two small kids. Seeing that so many of the security guys were happily married with families had Laz thinking about his own relationship.

He and Journey had been dating for almost two months and it had been the best months of Laz's life. Their work schedules made it a little challenging to get together every day, but so far they had succeeded. Even if it meant stealing away in a stairwell to share a kiss.

It amazed him that in just a short period of time, Journey had become such an important part of his life. Granted they still argued over stupid stuff, but it only attracted him to her that much more. They were good together, each balancing the other's strengths and weaknesses and Laz could definitely see a future with her.

Which was why he'd taken on more assignments with Supreme, moonlighting when he was off duty. He wanted to get his foot in the door so when he finally agreed to make a career change, he'd have a job lined up. Laz never thought he'd ever seriously consider leaving Atlanta PD, but he could definitely see that happening. Sooner than later. The pay was better. It was more flexible. And more importantly, the work so far seemed safer.

Once the meeting was over, Laz looked up to find Hamilton walking toward him.

"Hey, man. Thanks for agreeing to take on this last-minute assignment," he said, gripping Laz's hand and giving him a one-armed man hug. "I need to head to a meeting, but Kenton is upstairs and he'll give you the details."

They walked out together, but parted ways in the hallway and Laz took the stairs two at a time to the top floor where the offices were located. When he approached the executive assistant's door, Laz heard her giggling before he stepped in the doorway. Kenton was sitting on the edge of the desk, whispering something to the woman.

Laz cleared his throat, and Egypt practically leaped out of her seat while Kenton took his time standing to his full height. He narrowed his eyes at Laz as he buttoned his suit jacket.

The former FBI agent was a big guy who looked as if he should've been a linebacker for the Atlanta Falcons. He was also cool in every sense of the word. They'd worked together on a couple of small assignments and Laz had been impressed each time. The man had nerves of steel and had a calm about him that could easily ward off stressful situations.

"Am I interrupting?" Laz asked, trying not to laugh at the horrified look on Egypt's face. Her skin was too dark to determine if she was blushing, but the way she looked everywhere but at him was a sure sign that he'd interrupted something.

Kenton and Egypt. Interesting.

"Ready to head out?" Kenton asked as if nothing happened.

"Yeah, but Ham said that you'd give me details about the assignment. You want to do that now or on the way?"

"Since we have a little drive, on the way will work. We'll be meeting Angelo and Myles there."

Laz had sat on a government task force with Angelo, a former DEA agent, years ago and worked with him a few weeks ago after signing on with Supreme. He hadn't met Myles yet.

"Give me a minute," Kenton said, and Laz caught the hint and stepped out of the office. On his way out he heard Kenton ask Egypt if she was all right. Laz couldn't hear her reply, but did hear her tell Kenton to be careful out there.

"I'm always careful," Kenton said, and seconds later stepped into the hallway.

"So, you and Egypt, huh?" Laz asked as they headed down the back stairs toward the equipment room.

Kenton shrugged noncommittally. "She's a sweetheart,

but I've used my best moves on her. She's too concerned about fraternizing, though the company doesn't have a rule against it. She's not interested in being more than friends."

Laz would disagree based on what he saw a moment ago. Eyes didn't lie. The way Egypt had been looking at him once they pulled apart spoke volumes. She was interested. Besides, if she wasn't, she probably wouldn't have told him to be careful. Instead of telling him any of that, Laz kept his mouth shut. It wasn't any of his business and he wouldn't pretend to understand the workings of the female mind.

Once they had everything they needed, including covert ear pieces, they headed out back to the parking lot where the company vehicles were located.

"Tell me about this assignment."

"We're guarding James Halsted, an investment manager and CFO of Visioneering Investment Firm. He's been receiving threats after costing some investors over five million dollars."

Laz blew out a whistle as they climbed into one of the SUVs. "I guess that would piss somebody off." He wasn't used to being a passenger, but with Kenton's defensive driving skills, it made sense to have him behind the wheel.

"Yeah, I know, right? He has a speaking engagement tonight and wanted four guards. Angelo and Myles are responsible for getting him to and from the event, then you and I will help cover him while he's there."

An hour later, Laz identified one aspect of the job he didn't care much for. Standing around. Watching to ensure there were no threats or suspicious behaviors lurking nearby made for a long night.

Now they were following their client to a small stage that had been set up in the front part of the ballroom. Laz and Kenton stood a short distance behind him, while Angelo and Miles stood off to the side. Ten minutes into the man's speech and Laz wondered who had chosen James Halsted to be one of the featured speakers. The guy, with his Ben Stein monotone voice, was not only boring, but kept losing his place in his notes. Maybe he was nervous, but based on the audience's disinterested expressions, they didn't care either way.

"In closing," Halsted said, "I'd like to leave you with this, history has proven that you're better off paying a qualified investment manager to manage your financial affairs. If..."

Laz made eye contact with his team in preparation of walking Halsted off the stage and to the lobby. Originally their client had planned to stick around until the end of the event, but after receiving the threats, he'd decided to leave immediately after his presentation.

Laz and Kenton moved in sync, flanking the man as they headed to the lobby of the hotel. They had parked near a side door to make entering and departing the facility easier. He and Kenton stayed a step ahead of Halsted while Angelo and Myles pulled up the rear. Everything was fine until they got to the parking lot and a man leaped out from between two vans.

"Gun!" Laz yelled and the gunman disappeared between the cars, his hard footsteps echoing through the lot.

As planned, Angelo and Myles covered the client, making sure they got him to safety, and Laz and Kenton were responsible for pursuing and disarming the gunman.

"Go right," Laz mumbled to Kenton, who nodded and they split up. Adrenaline pumped through Laz's veins as he stayed low, slipping between cars searching for the man. They went up and down aisles, knowing the guy couldn't have gone far, but seeing him nowhere.

"Client is secured," Angelo said through the earpieces.

"Copy that," Kenton replied.

Hearing rustling to his left, Laz crotched down and spotted the perp's feet. He was hiding on the other side of a white sedan, and Laz whispered his position to Kenton as he eased up on the perp.

"Atlanta PD, drop your weapon!" Laz yelled.

The guy startled, turned and fired.

"Sonofa..." Laz dived behind a pickup truck just before

one of the windows shattered. When he heard the guy start running again, he went after him, staying low as he got closer. He saw Kenton moving parallel down the next aisle.

The guy fired again and kept moving until Laz cut through a set of cars and lunged.

"Oomph!" the man grunted when Laz landed on his back, his gun flying out of his hand.

"Stay still, asshole!" Laz ground out, breathing hard as he pressed his knee into the man's back and secured his hands behind him.

"You good, man?" Kenton asked Laz, after securing the perp's weapon.

"I'm good. Though I could've done without the excitement tonight."

Kenton laughed, and bent forward with his hands on his knees, breathing just as hard as Laz. "Don't front, you know you live for this high."

Laz chuckled, but didn't admit that the chase had been the highlight of the evening. He pulled out his cell phone and called for a pickup.

By the time they were done answering questions and getting their client home safely, it had been two o'clock in the morning. Add another forty-five minutes to get to Journey's place and Laz was dead on his feet.

"Hey," she said sleepily when she opened the door for him. Even with partially opened eyes, bed-hair, and no makeup, the sight of her still had blood rushing to the lower part of his body. His woman was sexy no matter the time of day, and Laz felt like the luckiest man alive.

"Hey, beautiful." He followed her into the dark foyer where he kicked off his shoes, setting them next to her small pile of expensive footwear. Next came his suit jacket which he hung in the coat closet.

Normally he would've pulled her into his arms and devoured her juicy lips, but even walking from the front door to her bedroom was taking effort.

He started for the bathroom, but realized she was in there and instead, mechanically went through his routine of getting undressed. After putting his gun in the top drawer of the nightstand, he stripped down to his boxer briefs, leaving the rest of his clothes wherever they landed.

Laz sat on the edge of the bed and just as he dropped back onto the mattress, the bathroom door opened.

"Ah, my poor baby," Journey said, standing next to the bed in a white sheer nightie that made his dick stir, but the rest of him couldn't move. "Don't tell me you're tired. I had big plans for you tonight."

"I'm sorry, babe. The night went longer than expected." There was a time when he could put in an eighteen-hour day and it would not wipe him out. But even with his gorgeous woman standing over him, looking good enough to eat, he couldn't drum up enough energy to move.

"Here, at least get further up on the bed so you can be comfortable." Journey helped him scoot up and when his head hit the pillow, it felt like laying on a cloud and he got lost in its softness.

Laz didn't know if he had dozed off, but the next thing he knew, Journey was straddling him.

"I *know* you must be tired. You didn't even kiss me when you came in."

"I'm sorry," he mumbled, enjoying the sweet, tender kisses she dropped onto his closed eyelids, then his cheek, and then onto his mouth. He opened for her when her tongue slipped between his lips and swept inside his mouth. Their tongues tangled, and her minty breath mingled with his, rousing something inside of him.

"I've missed you," she mumbled against his lips.

He didn't bother telling her that she had seen him that morning, and the day before that, and the day before that one. What man didn't want to hear his lady tell him that she missed him? Having her want to be with him as much, and as often, as he wanted to be with her was like a shot of adrenaline to his system.

Just like that of her sweet-smelling perfume. The tantalizing scent surrounded him as her mouth left his and she planted kisses down his heated skin.

"Feel free to have your way with me," he murmured with his eyes closed.

"Oh, I plan to," she said against his neck. Nipping at it, then sucking and no doubt marking him as her lower body ground against him.

Laz didn't care how wiped out he was, his body was loving this sweet torture. He sifted his fingers through her short tresses as he savored the feel of her mouth and hands on him. This was what he needed after a long day of work. His woman loving on him.

When her tongue swirled around one of his nipples, Laz released a long moan and his hands slid down her smooth thighs and rested on her hips. It didn't matter how tired he was, it was hard to resist a horny Journey. He loved when she was like this, taking what she wanted.

All those years of seeing her at work, looking totally professional and seizing every opportunity to verbally spar with him, he never knew this side of her. The side that enjoyed sex as much as he did.

When she stopped kissing on him, Laz's eyes eased open just as she removed the sheer garment from her body. His pulse increased. Even with half-opened lids, he zoned in on her full, tempting breasts. She had the type of body that could bring a dead man back to life.

With a hand on her back, Laz eased her forward, needing a taste of her. He palmed one of her breasts and brought it to his mouth. Tugging on her pert nipple, he sucked, licked and teased until he had her whimpering his name. Then he moved to the other one, giving it the same attention as the first one.

Journey moaned with each lap of his tongue, and the erotic sound she made when he grazed the sensitive tip with his teeth had his body stirring.

"Laz," she said breathily, and lifted slightly, causing her nipple to pop out of his mouth. "I need you out of your shorts," she said in a rush.

When his hands went for his waistband, apparently, he wasn't moving fast enough.

"Move." She swatted his hand aside. "I got you."

He couldn't help laughing. "Like I said, feel free to have your way with me, baby." She flashed him a wicked grin as she slid his shorts down his legs.

"Mmm… You claim to be exhausted, but there is one part of you that seems to be ready for action."

"Always." He sucked in a breath when her soft hand gripped him and then started sliding slowly up and down his length.

"I love how you're always ready for me, detective."

Laz grunted. "That sounds like one of my lines. I… Oh, sh…" His words were cut off when she slid down on him, her tightness squeezing his dick. She wasted no time before her hips started rotating. "Ah, baby. Damn…you feel good."

Leaning forward, her luscious breasts flattened against his chest as she captured his mouth in a searing kiss and continued moving the lower part of her body. If Laz wasn't awake before, he was definitely awake now.

He met her stroke for stroke while their bodies moved as one and their breathing increased. Laz already knew this would be a quickie, but as she increased the pace, his control started slipping. This was going to be quicker than he wanted.

On an erotic moan, Journey snatched her mouth from his. "Laz, I'm going to come," she panted, her hips moving faster as she squeezed her thighs, holding him tighter. When she lifted slightly, Laz's fingers dug into her hips and he slammed into her harder, going deeper with each thrust, loving how her breasts bounced in his face with each thrust.

"Laz!" she screamed, her head thrown back as an orgasm ripped through her.

The sight of her in the throes of passion only spurred him on and sent heat rippling beneath his skin. Within seconds, the turbulence of his release rocked him to his core and he surrendered to the erotic pleasure that overpowered him.

Journey collapsed on top of him, her arms spread out on either side of him. Their heavy breathing was the only sounds in the room. Neither of them moved for the longest time until Journey curled into him. No doubt she'd be asleep shortly.

Laz drummed up enough energy to roll to his side, and wrapped his arm around her to keep her close. When he pressed a kiss to the side of her sweat-slicked forehead, a peace filled him. "I love coming home to you," he murmured and his eyes drifted closed.

"Me too," she whispered just before he heard her soft snores.

Holding her like this, Laz knew for the first time in a long time what contentment felt like. At that moment, everything was right in his world.

Chapter Eighteen

Journey knocked on the district attorney's partially opened office door before pushing it open. She had gotten word that he needed to see her before she left for the day.

"You wanted to…" she started but stopped when she realized he was on the telephone. Before she could back out of the office, he lifted his hand and waved her in.

"I understand, commissioner. We appreciate your help in the matter. Okay…"

Giving him some privacy, Journey stood at one of the two windows that were on the opposite side of the room. Staring out at the courtyard below, she smiled thinking about Laz. They had fallen into such a comfortable routine, seeing each other every day. It was as if they'd been together for years. Starting their relationship as friends probably had a lot to do with how well they got along. But their connection was so strong it was almost scary. To think that she had come to depend on his presence in her life in such a short amount of time was mind-boggling.

"Sorry about that, Journey," the DA said after hanging up the phone. "Can you close the door?"

Journey did as requested before sitting in one of the leather chairs in front of his desk. She studied him as he sifted through a stack of files. Henry Gaines was one of the best bosses she'd ever had and he was loved by everyone in the office. Handsome, with short dark hair, expressive eyes with laugh lines, and the friendliest smile she'd ever seen on a man. He didn't look his sixty-plus years. Despite how stressful his job was, his demeanor rarely changed.

"Thanks for stopping by my office. I know you're trying to get out of here and start your weekend, but I wanted to talk to you before you left." He stared down at the file folder in his hand.

"O—kay," Journey said slowly wondering what this was about since he seemed a little distracted. He finally passed her the file, but before she could open it, he continued.

"I hope it goes without saying that whatever we discuss right now will remain in this office."

"Of course." Unease crept down her back. Rarely did he preface a conversation like that. Had he somehow found out she'd given Laz a heads-up about the Monsuli case?

Journey opened the file and her heart stalled. Her hands shook slightly before she set the opened file on her lap, willing herself to relax. *Okay, don't trip. This means nothing.* At least that's what she told herself as her attention remained on the folder's contents.

Case notes. *Enrique Monsuli.*

"I know this wasn't your case, but I wanted to talk to you about it. A couple of months ago, I thought for sure we had finally put this guy where he belonged—behind bars. But Monsuli is still insisting on his innocence and has hired a different lawyer to appeal his case."

Journey knew all of this because of whispers that had floated around the office. But relief flooded through her that Henry didn't seem the wiser about her conversation with Laz.

"Monsuli's new attorney claims our office withheld evidence that could have exonerated his client."

Journey had been skimming the file, but looked up at the last comment. "What?"

The withholding evidence claim surprised her. If nothing else, their office was thorough. Sure, it was possible something could've been missed, but she doubted it.

"The attorney is also saying that his defendant's trial was clouded by injustice and undermined by his trial lawyer."

"That's ridiculous. Maybe his lawyer did fail him, and I don't know all the details about the case, but I know Carmen is thorough. She and Prentice worked hard and made sure their case against Monsuli was solid," she said of the prosecutor who was a friend and Prentice, one of the DA's investigators. The two had worked tirelessly to ensure they put this guy away once and for all.

Henry smiled and sat back in his chair. "You don't have to tell me. Carmen is one of the best prosecutors we have. I know she did her job, but now we have to prove, again, that we have the right guy."

"Why are you telling me all of this, sir?"

He hesitated, tapping his pen rhythmically against the desk and then stopped. "You've always had a good relationship with the police department. Actually, better than most of our prosecutors. I'm wondering what you think of detectives Dimas and Chambers?"

Journey felt she knew Laz well, but she didn't know much about his partner, Ashton Chambers. That's what she told her boss. No way she was sharing information about her and Laz's relationship, but she highlighted his qualities as a detective.

"Detective Dimas is relentless in cleaning up these streets of people like Monsuli."

"Relentless enough to tamper with evidence?" Henry asked carefully. "That's one of the claims coming from the defense."

Journey shook her head. "No. Laz wouldn't tamper with evidence. I've called him out on some of his methods over the years, but he's a good detective, Henry. He wouldn't jeopardize his career by doing something like that."

"He's jeopardized his career more than any detective in their department, Journey. What makes you think he wou—"

"He wouldn't," she said with conviction, not missing the

way Henry's eyebrow lifted in question. He'd had dealings with Laz and apparently knew of some of his tactics, but Journey was willing to bet her career on Laz's innocence in this matter.

Henry nodded as if silently coming to some conclusion.

"Again, why have you brought this to my attention? Why aren't you having this conversation with Carmen or Prentice?"

"I have. They both agree with you. The problem is, since Carmen is on an indefinite medical leave, I need to reassign the case. Initially, I considered giving it to Gabe, thinking it would be a good assignment for him."

Oh no. That's the last person who should get the case.

"But then after speaking with him, talking to him the way you and I are doing, I don't think giving him the case is a good idea. He has some strong—and not necessarily good—opinions about some of the individuals involved in the case that concern me."

Yeah, I just bet. Journey had no idea where this was going, but she remained quiet.

"Between you and I, he feels Detective Dimas should be charged with obstruction of justice and tampering with evidence."

"What? That's insane!" Journey snapped, suddenly realizing how loud she'd gotten. "I'm sorry, sir, but how can Gabe come to that conclusion without having all the facts? I assume our office hasn't started investigating these new claims, have we?"

"Not in-depth, no, but I do have Prentice talking to some of the witnesses."

"I see. Does Gabe know this?" Journey asked, thinking that Gabe had probably heard whispers around the office about the case the way she had.

"He might, but at any rate, I trust your judgment, Journey, regarding the detective."

Henry had proven his trust in her a number of times when he'd asked her opinion about opposing parties, or legal processes. Normally those conversations centered around her own cases, not cases being overseen by other prosecutors in the office. She prayed he didn't ask her opinion about Gabe. She wouldn't be able to say anything good about the jerk.

"I know you and Detective Dimas have worked on many cases together. I'd like for you to take over the Monsuli case."

Journey stared at her boss, shocked by his request. "I can't!" she blurted before she could stop the words from flying out of her mouth.

Henry leaned forward and folded his forearms on the desk and studied her. "Care to tell me why you're refusing a case?"

Okay. Think. Think.

She knew why it wasn't a good idea. There were no rules about her dating a cop, but dating a person they were investigating might bring into question her moral principles. Anything that the investigation turned up, would she be able to keep her biases at bay? She didn't think so and the integrity of the case would be at risk.

Apprehension inched through her body. In her heart she believed Laz was innocent of any wrong doing, but what if he wasn't?

"Henry, I just don't know if me taking over Carmen's case is a good idea."

"Why?"

"Because...because based on the info that I just scanned in the case notes, and what I know of Lazarus, I think he's innocent of any wrongdoing as it relates to this case."

Henry smiled and sat back in his seat. "All the more reason for you to assume the case."

Journey frowned. "I don't understand."

"Sergeant Ford, Detective Dimas's CO, is one of my golfing buddies. I can't tell you the number of stories, and not all good, that I've heard about the detective. Ford often speaks of those who report to him, but not like he talks about Dimas. He respects his passion for the job, and his ability to help clean up our streets.

"But Journey, Monsuli is claiming that the vic was already dead when he arrived at the guy's office. He says he never saw a weapon and that the detectives showed up while he was there. He's still claiming that Detective Dimas is trying to frame him."

Journey shook her head. "From what I understand, the reports say that Monsuli was holding the weapon and there are witnesses."

"I understand all of that and I have no intention of pressing charges against Detective Dimas. At least not yet. The last thing I want is to send an innocent, decorated cop to jail. We just need to find the truth and make sure we have the right person behind bars. I'd like for you and Prentice to connect with Dimas and figure out all of this in the next thirty days. I'd also like the case handled without having to go back to court, and I believe you're the perfect person to pick up where Carmen left off."

This should be interesting.

*

Days later, Journey rode with Prentice to meet up with Laz to discuss the Monsuli case. Laz had been as shocked as she was when she told him about the conversation with the DA. His only concern was that Journey had been assigned the case.

According to him, Monsuli had recently orchestrated a few shady situations from behind bars, possibly threatening a couple of witnesses, but Laz couldn't prove it yet. He felt it was only a matter of time that the drug dealer might somehow try to get to her.

Journey knew he'd been thinking about Gwenn and what had happened with her. The last thing she wanted was for him to relive that dark time, and she tried reassuring him that she'd be fine. But it felt good to have someone besides her family worry about her. Yet, she didn't want him going all papa-bear on her.

"Explain to me why you want to focus more on the witnesses and the video footage evidence than the actual weapon," Prentice said, splitting his attention between her and the road as they discussed the Monsuli case.

"Actually, I'm still thinking about the weapon situation. There are two different reports. Our crime lab's report has that the victim's and Monsuli's DNA are on the weapon. For some reason, there's a second report that states that the weapon had been wiped, but they were able to get DNA matching the victim. They also have a partial print that supposedly belongs to Laz."

Journey closed the case file she'd been sifting through since getting into the car. She didn't believe Laz had tampered with the murder weapon, but she wanted to determine if they had enough evidence and witness testimony to keep Monsuli behind bars without bringing the weapon into question. And that's what she explained to Prentice.

But honestly, she didn't want to know the truth, and that bothered her. It would kill her to determine that Laz had indeed planted the knife. She was risking her professional integrity by not following some of the procedures she'd always followed during her career. Those same methods that set her apart from other prosecutors and got her answers when needed. Now because she was afraid of what would turn up, she didn't want to know.

Journey shifted in her seat and stared out the window. That nagging feeling that she was missing something was back. Even interviewing Laz's partner Ashton hadn't soothed her. Their recollection about the arrest was almost identical. Too identical. Making her think their stories had been rehearsed.

Journey mentally shook herself. She had to believe that Laz was being honest with her. She really wanted to believe him. But he'd lied about Gabe's beating. At least she was pretty sure he had, though he still hadn't admitted to it. What was to say he wasn't lying about this?

"There were two witnesses who claim to have seen Monsuli murder the victim," Prentice said, cutting into her thoughts. "One is now recanting his statement. Supposedly he's unsure of what he saw."

"What about the three who heard him threaten the guy the week prior to the murder? Have you had a chance to talk with them, ask them more questions?"

"The witness, Carol, Monsuli's former housekeeper, died of a heart attack early this morning."

"What? Oh my goodness. I hadn't heard." Journey reopened Monsuli's file that was still sitting in her lap. "She was only thirty-two. Did she have a history of heart problems or any health issues that you know of?"

"From what I understand, she was perfectly healthy. Her family is demanding an investigation. They think it was foul play. I'm meeting with the woman's sister tomorrow to find out why they think her death is suspicious. As for the witnesses who were in the building at the time of the murder, Laz was supposed to talk to one this morning and the other is not returning my calls."

Suddenly, the conversation Journey and Laz had, came to mind. Hopefully he wasn't right about Monsuli pulling strings from behind bars, but it was starting to look that way. She wasn't sure how deep this guy's organization went, but knew he was a very dangerous man.

"Rumor has it, Monsuli's second-in-command is kind of feeling himself now that he's running the organization. Maybe we can get word out that his boss might be released from jail. I'd think Mr. Second-in-command wouldn't be too happy to hear that if he's trying to move up the ladder."

"You're right. I'll see if Laz has any connections that might be able to spread the word to the right people."

Seemed Laz had a way with people, and not all were good law-abiding citizens, if Gabe's beating was any indication.

Chapter Nineteen

A short while later Journey and Prentice arrived at the cafe. As they waited for Laz, anxiousness fluttered inside her gut. Normally they'd talked or texted throughout the day and had spent every night together, but for the last three nights Laz had been working a twelve-hour, third-shift surveillance case.

Considering she wasn't the clingy type, she missed him like crazy.

A tickling sensation on the back of Journey's neck had her looking up just as Laz entered the cafe. Warmth spread through her body when their gazes connected.

Good Lord.

The man was a walking billboard for everything lethal and sexy. His hair—which seemed to grow an inch every day—was pulled away from his face and bound at his nape. She loved a man with a little scruff on his face and Laz wore the look well. It appeared he hadn't shaved since the last time she'd seen him, giving him a rugged appearance.

Other patrons in the restaurant took notice as he made his way toward them. Not because of the way the tan T-shirt he wore stretched across his broad chest showed off his thick arms and wide shoulders. No. The police badge hanging from a silver chain around his neck stood out like a blinking red streetlight. Or it could've been the way his thick legs, encased in dark jeans, were emphasized by the thigh-strapped gun holster he sported. That only added to his hotness. A man in almost any type of uniform turned her on, and Laz's relaxed work look was no different.

Journey had to control the impulse to go and greet him with a kiss, one that matched the desire raging through her body. Instead, she reached for her glass of water and took a huge gulp. When what she really wanted to do was put the cold glass to the side of her face to help cool her off. They hadn't discussed how they would greet each other when in public, but she planned to follow his lead.

"Hey, sorry I'm late." Laz slid into the booth next to her, sending her temperature through the roof. Every nerve in her body was on high alert. "Did you guys order already?"

God, he smells good. A light sage and woodsy scent that was uniquely him. Sitting this close to Laz, not being able to kiss or touch him was going to kill her.

"Not yet, we just arrived not too long ago," Journey managed to say, her voice hitching on the last word due to his hand moving to her thigh.

She glanced at him, her heart practically beating out of her chest at the bold move. He had to know that she was already wound tight from not seeing him. How could he in good conscience torture her by sitting so close and worse, caressing her bare thigh?

"Hey," he said, his voice low and husky, and his gaze on her mouth.

Heat rose to her face. Had her skin not been as dark as it was, no doubt her cheeks would be glowing red. As it was, her panties were getting wetter by the minute and all he'd done was touch her thigh and say hey.

"Hi," she croaked and looked away, only to make eye contact with Prentice, who glanced between her and Laz before the corners of his lips curled upward.

Okay, this is weird.

Only her sister, Ashton, and a few of Laz's closest

friends knew they were dating. Journey wasn't sure she wanted anyone else to know just yet, especially those in the DA office—mainly because of the Monsuli case. She was always professional and carried herself as such, but Laz's behavior, on the other hand, was often questionable, and uncontrollable. Like with those in law enforcement who knew him, individuals in her office either liked him or hated his guts. Gabe was a prime example of the latter.

Just relax, she told herself several times, finding no relief in the silent command. She just had to get through their meal without making a fool of herself.

Once the server took their orders, conversation flowed easily. Journey listened as Laz and Prentice discussed an upcoming Atlanta Braves game. On the day she had told Laz about her being assigned the case, she'd learned that he and Prentice had worked together in the past before Prentice started working for the DA's office.

The server brought their meals to them in record time, and Journey didn't miss the way the woman, a pretty blonde with intense blue eyes and pouty lips, eyed Laz with interest. He didn't seem to notice how she batted her long eyelashes and smiled brightly each time he said something to her. Knowing Laz, he had noticed but just didn't acknowledge the woman's interest.

"Did you guys know that Carmen's car accident wasn't an accident?" Laz asked.

"What?" Journey and Prentice said in unison.

Journey wiped her mouth with her napkin. "Are you saying someone intentionally caused her accident?"

"I looked at the official report last night. It was determined that her brake lines were cut."

"Oh my God," Journey mumbled. "I knew she was on medical leave, but I had no idea..."

Laz gave her leg a gentle squeeze. "I tagged along with the detective on the case to her house and she almost passed out when she heard the news. When we tried questioning her, she shut down saying she didn't know anyone who would want to hurt her."

"You think she was lying," Prentice said as more of a statement than a question.

"Yeah. We'll check her phone records and gather as much information as we can to determine if someone has threatened her. She was pretty anxious for us to leave and was acting nervous even before she found out about the brakes."

"Prentice, who checked the weapon out of lockup for the trial?" Journey asked, pushing her rice around on her plate, no longer hungry. She couldn't remember seeing that information in the case notes.

"I was supposed to get it out of evidence before the trial, but received a call from Carmen that morning saying that she'd take care of it." He studied Journey. "You don't think Carmen had anything to do with tampering with the evidence, do you?"

Journey set her fork down and rubbed her temples. "Right now, I'm not putting anything past anyone." Including Laz. Going forward, she planned to treat this case like any other. She just hoped he was being honest with her.

They discussed next steps, each taking on different tasks. Journey needed to talk to Carmen, who she suspected knew more than she'd shared in her notes. If Monsuli had threatened her or any of their witnesses, Journey planned to find out.

Laz glanced at his watch. "All right, you guys. I need to get back to work."

They took care of the bill and headed for the door. When they stepped outside and into the parking lot, Laz wrapped his arm around Journey's waist.

"Prentice, man, can you give us a second?" Laz asked.

"Yeah, take all the time you need. I'll be in the car."

With a hand at the small of her back, Laz guided Journey a few feet away from the entrance of the cafe.

He backed her against the building, his large body blocking her and her view of the parking lot.

"Are you okay? Towards the end there, you seemed a bit distracted," he said, searching her eyes.

"The news about Carmen was a little disturbing, and I keep thinking about you saying that Monsuli had a long reach."

"That's why I need you to be extra-vigilant about being careful, Journey. I think he got to Carmen. I don't know how or when, but we'll figure it out. You just need to remember that the guy is capable of anything."

When she glanced away, Laz touched her hip, forcing her attention back to him.

"I've missed you."

"I've missed you, too. Am I going to see you tonight?" she asked, her hands on his chest, loving how his muscles contracted beneath her touch.

"Yeah, but it might be late."

"It doesn't matter the time. I want to see you." She had never considered herself or wanted to be one of those needy women, but tonight she needed him. It also seemed she got a better night's sleep when they shared a bed.

Laz studied her without responding right away. "You sure you're okay?"

"Oh yeah, I'm fine. I just... I just need you tonight. If you can't come by, I'll understand."

He placed a finger under her chin and lifted her head. "I'll be there, but you'd tell me if something was wrong, right?"

She nodded, though the case had her anxious. Not just because of the new development about Carmen, but also because Journey didn't know what she'd do if Laz wasn't being honest with her. He meant so much to her and she needed him to be innocent of any wrongdoing as it related to this case.

"Did I tell you how sexy you look today?"

Journey smiled and glanced down at her pinstriped suit. "You always say that." The suit molded over her figure. And the skirt, with its peek-a-boo split, was a little daring for work, but the outfit always made her feel sexy and powerful.

"I always mean it. But today, I can't help but think that you wore this little number for me, giving me access to your silky thigh."

"You're so bad. I almost knocked over my drink in there when your hand slid under my skirt and inched up my leg."

Laz shrugged. "I couldn't help myself. At least I stopped. I was tempted to go all the way up and inside your panties."

"Who said I was wearing panties?"

"See, you know what?"

Journey laughed at the face he made. "Hey, you started it."

"And I plan on finishing it tonight. Now give me some love. I have to get going."

When their lips connected, it was as if all the background noise disappeared and they were the only two people on earth. This man had eased into her life, and now had such a big chunk of her heart.

"Are you heading home?" he asked when they finally pulled apart.

"Not yet. I need to go back to the office for a little while, and then I'll head home." It was almost five o'clock, but she had at least a couple of more hours of work.

"All right, be safe and shoot me a text when you get home," he said as he escorted her to Prentice's car.

"Yeah, yeah, I know the drill." He was such a worrywart, but if she were honest, she liked that he cared about her safety.

Laz squeezed her hand and opened the passenger side car door. "Take care of her," were his parting words to Prentice before he closed the door and walked away from the vehicle.

"So, you and Laz, huh?" Prentice grinned. "Didn't see that one coming, but I couldn't miss the way you glared at the server. I thought you were going to stab her with your fork at the way she was checking Laz out."

Journey laughed. "Stop. I was not that bad," she said

smiling from ear to ear, giddiness swirling inside of her. She felt like a high schooler with her first crush as she told Prentice that the relationship was pretty new. Journey also mentioned wanting to keep it quiet around the office, at least until they finished the Monsuli case. "I know you and Laz worked together a bit in the past. What do you think of him?"

"He's a good guy. A little high-strung, but if I ever wanted someone to have my six, it would be him."

"Do you think he's capable of planting evidence?"

After a short hesitation, he said, "Yeah, I do. Whether or not he did that in the Monsuli case, I don't know, but I wouldn't put anything past him."

Journey's heart sank. "How can you say that you'd want him to be the one watching your back when, if I'm hearing you right, he's just as much of a criminal as the ones he gets off the streets?"

She had asked herself more than once: out of all of the men in the city, why'd she have to fall for him?

"Journey, Laz is…complicated. He has his own set of rules that he lives by. I actually admire him. He always gets his man…or woman." Prentice grinned. "Seriously though, Laz gets the job done and if you get in his way…" Prentice shrugged. "Let's just say, he will trample you. Rules be damned. He doesn't fit into some tidy little morally correct box. So if that's what you're looking for, he's not your guy."

Without commenting, Journey turned to the passenger side window.

But he is my guy.

Chapter Twenty

"Journey thinks you tampered with the evidence, huh?" Ashton asked.

Laz put his cell phone on speaker as he tied his black tie. Normally he wasn't a fan of wearing a suit and tie, but according to Journey, he looked hot in them. Tonight, a couple of A-list actors were renting out the large VIP section at Club Masquerade and Mason wanted extra security on hand. Laz had been doing more and more moonlighting for Supreme whenever he was off duty.

"She hasn't said that, but I have a feeling she's been thinking about it," Laz said, slipping into his jacket.

"So she doesn't trust you?"

Last week when he met with Journey and Prentice at the cafe, Laz was pretty sure she was struggling with what to believe as it related to him and the case. Even that night, the way she hung onto him when he first arrived at her place, all types of warning bells went off in his head.

It was as if she was afraid to let him go. Afraid she'd lose him.

Since then she seemed her normal, secure self, but still he wondered.

"Journey has every right to be leery of anything I tell her," Laz finally said to Ashton. "She has had plenty of dealings with me when it comes to my cases, and as a smart woman, I'm sure she knows I only share what I want her to know."

"Are you going to tell her the tru—"

"I've told her everything I'm going to say about me, you, and the Monsuli case. But right now, I need to head to the club."

"Okay, before you go, what did Journey say about offering Melody Kane witness protection if she agrees to testify?"

"She's hoping Monsuli's case doesn't go back to trial," he finally said. "But if it does, her office is prepared to offer Melody a whole new identity."

"Good to hear, but let's hope this doesn't go back to trial. Then we can be done with Monsuli once and for all."

"Yeah, let's hope."

After disconnecting the call, Laz finished dressing. Earning Journey's trust was important to him, but when it came to how he handled cases, he wasn't sure if he could trust her with the truth all the time. He never wanted to put her in a compromising position to where she had to choose him over the law. That's why he was planning to turn in his badge once the Monsuli case was wrapped up. He was finally ready for the next chapter of his life, and those plans included building a life with Journey.

First, he needed to prove to her that he had changed his ways. Hopefully, the changes he had planned would do just that.

Hopefully.

Hours later, Laz was done working and strolled through the first floor of Club Masquerade and headed toward the exit. If all went as planned in the next couple of months, he would work with Supreme Security full-time. He looked forward to being one of Atlanta's finest, as Mason had called his growing group of police officers who worked for the agency.

"Excuse me," one of the servers said when she bumped

into Laz, carrying a tray of drinks.

"No problem, sweetheart."

Laz moved around the oversized circular bar where people were sipping their drinks, talking and laughing, while others bobbed their heads to a popular hip-hop song. Even at midnight, he wasn't surprised that people were still strolling into the club. The place was a hot spot in Atlanta, and it looked as if business was better than ever.

Laz stepped outside, the air cool but comfortable. He loosened his tie, noticing the line of people still waiting to get into the club had died down some, but still hosted at least twenty-five people. There was also a line of cars waiting to valet. The car at the front of the line, a BMW, caught his attention. Not because it was a shiny white seven-series BMW, but because of the man who stepped out of it.

They made eye contact and as usual, every muscle in Laz's body tightened.

Attorney Gabriel Hall. The sight of him immediately brought back the memory of how the guy had manhandled Journey. There had always been something about Hall that never sat right with Laz. He was a little too slick. Always strutting around as if he was God's gift to the world.

That's why Laz had him under surveillance. Now it was only a matter of time before Gabriel Hall got all that was coming to him.

"Detective," Hall said after he accepted a ticket from the valet and moved toward the front of the building where Laz had stopped.

"Counselor," Laz said dryly, the adrenaline in his body quickly amping up as the man stood next to him.

"Kind of an upscale club for someone like you, isn't it? I figured you for more of a corner-bar kind of guy. Then again, I guess if you're screwing a *certain* prosecutor then maybe yo—"

"Be careful, man." The lethalness behind Laz's words caught the attention of those nearby if the *oohs* were any indication.

Hall laughed, the sound grating down Laz's spine. The last thing he needed right now was to let this guy goad him into doing something stupid.

"Have a good night, counselor." Laz turned, but hadn't taken two steps before Hall spoke again.

"What? You don't want me talking about your woman? No problem. I'm done with her anyway. My only regret is that I should've fucked her when I had a chance. Maybe when they haul your ass to jail, I'll corner her in the office and…"

Laz didn't even feel himself move. All he saw was red as he slammed his fist into Gabe's face, and then pounded him, jabbing him in his chest, his ribs. Punching him everywhere he knew would cause the most pain. Making every lick count.

"I will kill you if you ever go near her." Laz vaguely heard the screams, whoops, and hollering from those nearby as he continued Gabe's punishment. The thought of the man trying to force himself on Journey someday made Laz hit him harder.

"Man, get off of him!" Hamilton's voice pierced the haze in Laz's head as his friend pulled him off of Hall, practically lifting him off the ground. Hamilton didn't release him until they were several feet away. "You have lost your damn mind!" he fumed, standing directly in Laz's face.

He spewed a few more words, but Laz tuned him out. Aware of the sirens in the distance, his gaze went to Hall who was laying unmoving on the ground. Several of the club's security team tended to him as a crowd formed around him.

"Damn it, Laz. You already know they're going to haul your ass—"

"I'll turn myself in," Laz said, finishing Hamilton's sentence. He knew he had just fucked up, but it was too late to care.

"I can tell you now, Mason is not the type to give you too many chances. You better get your shit together and work on your temper. What I just saw back there…isn't going to fly. You feel me?"

Laz nodded as Hamilton continued his rant, but at the moment, all he could think about was Journey. He couldn't lose her. Not over this. But he had promised her that he wouldn't do anything to embarrass her or taint her reputation.

But this…this was bad. If she kicked his ass to the curb it would serve him right.

*

"What have you done?"

Laz lifted his head from the cot he was laying on when he heard Journey's voice. Seeing her on the other side of the jail bars made him feel worse than he already did, knowing how disappointed she'd be.

He placed his feet on the floor then stood, moving slowly to the bars. "I assume that's a rhetorical question since I have a feeling you know what I've done." His curt response only made her angrier. And she was definitely mad if the way she narrowed her eyes and balled her fists at her sides were any indication.

"Laz," she said through gritted teeth. "I am furious with you right now. It's a good thing you're in there and I'm out here. I can't believe you put the man in the hospital," she whispered when others in nearby cells grew silent. The arresting officer had placed him in one of the interrogation rooms, but Ford had him moved to one of the holding cells. Told him that if he wanted to act like a criminal, that's exactly how he would be treated.

"When Hamilton tried bailing you out, why did you insist on staying? That doesn't make any sense."

"The streets aren't safe for Hall if I walk out of here." He knew himself well enough to know when he was out of control, and the way he was feeling, jail was the best place for him right now.

"Laz, you're one of the sweetest people I know. How—"

"Don't get it twisted, Journey. I'm not *that* guy. I meant what I said to Hall. I will fucking kill him if he comes near you again."

"Stop it! Stop talking like that or you'll be spending more than a day in here." She shook her head and he stiffened when he saw her eyes water. He hadn't seen her cry since that night she was attacked and he never wanted to see tears in her eyes again unless they were happy ones.

But then Laz looked at her, really *looked* at her, noting her red, droopy eyes and ashen skin. Her face looked thinner, too. Granted, it was the middle of the night, and she had probably been asleep, but something seemed off with her. Now that he thought about it, she had stayed in bed a little later than usual that morning. He assumed she was tired because of her long work days, but maybe she was sick.

"You feelin' okay?" he asked, stretching his hand through the bars to touch her forehead, but she swatted him away.

"How can you even ask me that? Of course, *I'm not okay!*" she snapped.

The anger in her eyes would've brought a weaker man to his knees, but not him. He'd been on the receiving end of those daggers that she often shot him, more times than he could count.

With her arms wrapped around her midsection, she paced in front of the cell. "Sometimes...sometimes I don't understand you, Laz. I have tried. God knows I've tried, but..."

Unease crawled through Laz's body at the anguish and defeat in her tone. He hoped she wasn't giving up on him. They were going great, getting to know each other and really making a go at their relationship. He loved her more than he'd ever be able to express and he couldn't lose her, especially not because of Hall.

"What are you saying, Journey?"

She scowled at him with her hands planted on her hips. "I'm saying that I'm so pissed at you right now I could—"

"You could what?" He moved as close to her as the bars would allow. Grasping the front of her jacket, he gently tugged her as close as he could get her. "You could what?

Kiss me? Make love to me? You already know that when you're mad at me, it's a serious turn-on."

"Laz, *this* is serious. Do you have any idea of how much trouble you're in? Do you?"

He released her. Yes, he knew. No doubt he would be charged with a minimum of assault and knowing Hall, probably a few other charges.

"You threatened *and* assaulted a government official. That's a Class C felony at best and a fe-de-ral..." she said slowly, "...crime, Laz. I'm talking FBI involvement."

"Damn it, Journey! You think I don't know all of that?"

What could he say? If he had it to do all over again, he'd probably do everything the same. There was no way he was going to let that asshole disrespect her. And the thought of Hall even thinking about putting his hands on her again made Laz crazy. "You didn't hear him, Journey. You didn't hear what he said."

"I don't give a crap what Gabe said. I already told you I can handle him."

"No you can't, Journey!" Laz yelled. "I'm sick of you saying that shit. I know men like him. He thinks he can do and say whatever the hell he wants and then hide behind his position in the DA's office." Laz got louder with each word.

One of the officers came back and before he could say anything, Laz said, "We're good, Kevin." The cop nodded and left them alone again.

"Oh, so like you do whatever the hell you want, and say whatever you want and hide behind your gun and your badge? Sounds like you and Gabe are a lot alike."

"Don't! Don't you dare put him and me in the same category. I would never put my hands on a woman to inflict pain. You or no one else in this world has ever heard of me hurting or disrespecting a woman. Never! So don't put me in the same category with that bastard."

*

He was right, Journey thought. He and Gabe might've both been arrogant, stubborn, and a host of other adjectives, but she had never heard of Laz mistreating a woman.

Gabe, on the other hand, was a whole different story. Though she hoped it wasn't the case, she wouldn't be surprised to hear that he had harassed other women in their office.

Journey turned and leaned her back against the bars, her arms folded across her chest. Laz remained quiet, but she felt his presence immediately behind her. At least he had sense enough not to touch her right now. She might've been in love with him, but there was no way she could approve of this type of behavior.

He gripped the bars on each side of her, his warm breath near her ear sending a shiver through her body. "Baby, I'm sorry. You know I would never do anything to intentionally hurt you or disappoint you. I didn't mean for any of this to happen, but I couldn't let him talk about you like that. His words…his intent…they got to me. He made it sound like he…"

Journey tuned him out. All she could think about was how she knew getting involved with Laz was risky, but this? This was ridiculous. And no matter how stupid the situation he'd gotten himself into, she wanted to wrap her arms around him and never let go. How crazy was that?

Lucky for him, there were witnesses who heard what Gabe had said about her. If Laz was officially charged, his motive for threatening to kill Gabe would be taken into consideration. She was determined to do whatever she needed to get Laz out of this. No matter the cost. And then she needed to decide if there was a future for them.

She pushed away from the bars, barely sparing him a glance as she walked away. "I'll talk to you later," she said over her shoulder.

"Wait. Where are you going?"

Journey stopped and huffed, then slowly moved back to his cell. She wasn't as mad as when she first walked in, but seeing him behind bars pained her. She needed to get her head back on straight and the longer she was there, the more she felt as if she was losing herself.

"Talk to me. Where are you going?"

"Since you prefer to sit in jail, what I do going forward is no longer your business." Laz jerked back as if she had slapped him, but didn't respond. "Goodbye, Laz."

Though it was one of the hardest things she'd ever done, she walked away despite him calling out to her.

"I need to go back to taking care of me," she mumbled to herself.

But first there was something she needed to take care of once and for all. Something she should have handled months ago.

Chapter Twenty-One

The next morning, Journey knocked once before pushing open Gabe's hospital room door, not prepared for what she saw. He was almost unrecognizable with the number of bruises on his face and his left eye swollen shut. Add those injuries to his fractured ribs and it was safe to say he was in some serious pain.

"What do you want? Plan to pick up where your boyfriend left off?" he spat, looking at her as if she was the lowest form of human life. "If you came to plead his case, don't bother. I want his ass in prison for a long time for what he's done to me."

Instead of getting in the bed early to fight whatever bug was attacking her immune system, Journey had worked most of the night. Then she was in the office before the sun came up to prepare for this conversation.

"I don't think you want to press charges, Gabe," she finally spoke.

"Like hell. Do you see what he did to me?" He pointed at his face. "If I could prove he had something to do with me getting jumped weeks ago, I'd tack that onto the current charges against him."

She had no doubt that Gabe planned to dig up as much dirt as he could on Laz. What she had planned had to work.

158

At least she hoped.

"I just don't understand you," Gabe continued. "You and I could've been so good together. Not only would we have made a good-looking couple, but we could've been one of the most powerful couples in the city. Instead you end up with that jerk. Don't you want better for yourself?"

Journey was too nauseated and exhausted to list all the ways that Laz was more of a man than he could ever dream of being. Besides that, she couldn't believe that Gabe was still hanging onto his infatuation with her. She had never disliked someone as much as she did him, and there was no way they could have ever gotten together.

Instead of speaking, she held up a twenty-five-page document in one hand and a flash drive in the other before letting them both fall back to her side. She had decided that morning to treat this conversation like one of her closing arguments, dramatics and all.

Gabe looked at her warily, as if afraid to ask what was going on. When he didn't ask, she explained.

"For the past few months, I have tolerated you getting in my face, talking crazy and harassing me. I didn't report you because I was hoping that whatever was going on with you would pass. But then you crossed the line when you put your hands on me." Still he remained quiet. "If you don't drop the charges against Laz, several things will happen. I will move forward in filing sexual harassment charges against you, and I have proof."

She held up the flash drive. Laz had gotten a copy of the courthouse tape that had footage of her encounter with Gabe. He'd given it to her days after the incident, encouraging her to use it to get rid of Gabe once and for all. Just recently, he had given her more ammunition to use against him.

Gabe chuckled but stopped and groaned, one hand going to his face, the other to his ribs. "You do know blackmailing someone is a crime, right? You really have stooped to your man's level. My answer is no. I'll argue against whatever is on that drive."

"Funny thing is, you and Laz could probably share a jail cell." Journey lifted the papers in her hand. "I have documented—complete with dates, times, and in some cases, pictures—of fifteen instances of you involved in drug dealings. Either as a user or a seller, depends on how an observer regards the photos. Oh, wait, I forgot to mention. You've been under surveillance."

Gabe's features hardened, but he remained quiet.

Those late nights recently, when Journey thought Laz had been working a case, he was following Gabe. The pictures he'd given her would not only cost Gabe his job, but his law license as well. And depending on how some of the photos were interpreted, and whether he had a good attorney, he could do time in jail.

She held up the stack of papers and the flash drive. "I really don't care what you do in your spare time. But your conduct lately has been deplorable. You have not only been mistreating me, but you have disgraced the DA's office with your extracurricular activities. You've been walking around this city like you're untouchable. Behaving worse than the people we put away. I have no other choice but to step in and do something."

"Something like what?"

"Actually, I'm going to give you a chance to get your life together, Gabe. I think everyone deserves a second chance. In the next two weeks, I want you to get help. I have a referral list of rehab places all ready for you, and I also want you to leave Georgia and never come back."

"Now you're talking crazy. I don't know what all you have on me, but I'll fight it."

"Really? I'm not one to judge, but the picture of you in the park—after midnight—with your pants down around your ankles could really be damaging to your career. Do you really want me to release this video and the hundreds of photos I have of you and your misconduct?"

Journey tapped the flash drive against her cheek as she

pretended to be in deep thought.

She hated stooping to this level. Hated that she allowed Laz to put her in this position, but she couldn't let him go to jail for defending her. Especially knowing what type of person Gabe was.

"Maybe you should dig back through your memory bank. Think Piedmont Park late one night a few weeks ago." She shook her head. "Those photos alone are enough to let me know that I was right not to ever get involved with you. And there are so many more instances documented. You're lucky I'm giving you a chance to get out of town. You're being given an opportunity to get help for your drug problem. Oh, and I will be keeping track of your progress."

When he remained quiet, Journey continued.

"Or you can stick around and find out what happens. Not only will the DA kick you out on your ass, but you'll be disbarred. Not to mention the negative media attention you're going to receive. Are you sure going after Laz is worth it?"

"I can't believe you're threatening me," he seethed.

Yeah, she couldn't believe it either.

Maybe that part of Laz that skated on the edge of right and wrong had rubbed off on her, and it scared Journey to death. She always followed the rules. Always made sure in all of her professional dealings that she obeyed the law to the letter. But if playing a little dirty got Laz out of trouble, and freed her of Gabe's harassment, so be it. The arrogant jerk had made her work life hell for months, and it was past time she put a stop to it.

"Don't think of this as a threat, Gabe. Think of it as me giving you a heads-up on my future plans. It's up to you to accept what I'm...proposing, or not. But once I walk out of here, the offer is off the table."

*

Sitting in Ford's office, waiting for him to return from a meeting, Laz thought about the last week of his life.

He didn't know why Hall had dropped the charges against him, but he had a feeling Journey had something to do with it. Maybe she had finally used the information he'd given her regarding Hall, revealing his extracurricular activities. Unfortunately, Laz hadn't been able to find out for sure her involvement since she wouldn't take his calls.

After trying to reach her several times over the past few days and getting her voicemail, she had finally answered his call late last night. Laz couldn't say that he was surprised by her coldness, but it felt like a stab to the chest when she told him they needed a break. The whole conversation barely lasted two minutes before she said goodbye. Not only didn't he get a chance to question her about Hall, but he also didn't get the chance to tell her that he loved her.

Sitting in jail had given him plenty of time to think about how the last few months had been some of the best of his life with Journey. Spending time with her every day and most of their nights together felt like the most natural thing in the world to him.

That's what he wanted going forward. She was who he wanted in his life.

With that decision made, he knew for sure he had to make some changes. The day of his release, he had returned to the anger management group that he had participated in off and on for the last few years.

He had also smoothed things over with Mason Bennett.

After explaining what went down with Gabe, Laz was being given a second chance to prove that he would make a good addition to the Atlanta's finest team.

Now he was sitting in Ford's office waiting to do something he should've done years ago.

"Usually when someone is suspended, they don't show up at work," Ford said as he walked into his office, slamming his door closed. He dropped down in his desk chair, ignoring the way it protested under his weight. "What are you doing here, Laz?"

"I came to apologize."

Ford's left brow lifted in disbelief. "Well, that's a first. All the shit you've pulled over the years and *now* you want to apologize?'"

Laz shrugged nonchalantly. "Well, I'm not sorry for most of that, but I am sorry for putting you in some compromising positions, especially this situation recently. Though I had good reason for what I did to Hall, I probably could've handled the situation better." Laz threw up his hands. "But I won't rehash all of that. I just want you to know that I have appreciated your support over the years."

"Why do I have a feeling this little impromptu meeting is about more than an apology?"

Due to his suspension, Laz had already turned in his badge and service weapon. He set his letter of resignation in the middle of Ford's desk. "You're finally going to be rid of me." He grinned at Ford's frown.

"Why now?"

"It's time. Hell, it's past time. I'm actually surprised you haven't fired my ass before now."

Ford chuckled. "Oh, I've thought about it more than once and had even started the paperwork at least a hundred times, but you're a damn good cop, Laz. Shady as hell, but damn good."

Laz laughed and stood. "Thanks, I think. Sorry for all the trouble, Sarg."

"No you're not." Ford stood and extended his hand. "You'll be missed, Lazarus. All the best to you, man."

"Thanks, and if you ever need me to do any, um…let's just say, heavy lifting for you guys, you know where to find me."

After saying his goodbyes to everyone, Laz left the precinct feeling lighter than he'd felt in a long time.

His next assignment with Supreme Security wasn't for another week, giving him time to get his personal life in order. He had to win Journey and her trust back. She wasn't making it easy for him, but he was up for the challenge.

Chapter Twenty-Two

Journey shoved her cell phone into the side pocket of her handbag and released a noisy sigh. Staring out the passenger side window as her sister drove her back to work, she wondered if agreeing to meet with Laz later had been a good idea. It didn't matter that she'd thought about him practically every hour of every day since leaving him behind bars. She wasn't ready to see him.

"You should've just told him, Journey," Geneva said as she maneuvered the car through downtown traffic. "You're working yourself into a tizzy for no reason. He—"

"No reason!" Journey snapped. "You're acting like I just stubbed my toe or something. My life is about to change...forever! Nothing will ever be the same. Not my life. Not my body. Nothing!"

Journey covered her face with her hands and growled. She had royally screwed up. Something she rarely did. She planned everything, but this...

"Maybe you should go home instead of going back to work. Clearly you need some rest."

"I can't. I'm swamped. I can barely keep up with my work load, and don't even get me started about my crazy work hours. All the more reason why I can't handle any more responsibilities."

"Are you done?"

"No, I'm not done." Journey sagged against her seat, trying to fight the tears that had been threatening to fall ever since she walked out of the doctor's office. "How am I going to tell Laz that...that..." She was never at a loss for words, but she'd been having trouble with these particular words.

Words she never thought she'd ever have to say.

"You open your mouth and say, *I'm pregnant, Laz.* Three little words. Or you can just say—*we're having a baby.* Oh, I know. You can take a more comical route and say something like—*How would you feel about being my baby's daddy?* Or, you know what? If that doesn't work for you, you can say..."

Journey shook her head, unable to keep the smile from her lips as her sister continued with one scenario after another, getting sillier with each one. "Sometimes I can't stand you," Journey mumbled, swiping at an errant tear.

"Whatever. You know you *love* me," Geneva said as she pulled up to the side entrance of the courthouse.

"This is the scariest thing I've ever had to face. I don't know how to be somebody's mother, Geneva."

"You love kids."

"Yeah, when they belong to someone else. Raising a child, as a single mom, is hard for women who have that mommy...compassionate gene. But for those of us who don't have that trait, like me, what am I supposed to do? What if I screw up and...and..."

"Would you knock it off! Instead of going to see your OB/GYN, maybe you should've gone to get your head checked. You are straight trippin'. Just because having a baby wasn't on that *ridiculous* master to-do list you live by doesn't mean you can't handle it. Or is it that you're thinking about the alternative?"

Journey gasped. "Of course not! I couldn't...ever!"

"All right then. You're going to handle motherhood like you handle everything else. Like a damn maniac who has to do everything perfectly."

"You're not helping, Geneva."

"Sorry. Anyway, you're forgetting about one important factor."

"What's that?"

"Laz. That man worships the ground you walk on. When he finds out that you're having his baby, he probably won't let your feet touch the ground. He's going to be thrilled. Almost as thrilled as I am about becoming an auntie."

"Still not helping. The thought of either of you helping me raise this baby makes me even more nervous. You both live life on the edge. You both curse *way* too much. And you both get on my last nerve." Journey shook her head in mock disgust. "With you two, I might not survive any of this."

Geneva laughed. "Shut up. We're not that bad." She paused. "Okay, maybe we are. But seriously, sis. I know you've had these grand career plans for all of your life. Having a baby or two doesn't mean you can't still be the DA or a judge someday. No, it probably won't be easy, but you are the most determined woman I know. I have no doubt you're going to accomplish all of your goals while being an amazing mommy."

More tears welled up in Journey's eyes and she dug through her bag for tissue. "I hate it when you say stuff like that. You almost sound…human."

Geneva laughed again. "Actually, I almost gagged on those words. Now get your ass out of my car so I can get back to work."

Journey reached over and hugged her little sister. "Even if you are a pain in the you-know-what, I love you. Thanks for dropping everything to pick me up from the doctor's office. I really appreciate it."

"No problem, but you should've called Laz to pick you up. That would've been the perfect time to spring this exciting news on him."

"Maybe."

"When you see him tonight, tell him."

"Yeah, yeah." Journey climbed out of the car and started to walk away but turned back when her sister rolled down the window and called out her name.

"What?"

"I want to be there when you tell Mom and Dad the news. I want to see their faces when they find out their perfect daughter is having a baby out of wedlock."

Journey shook her head. "Like I said, I can't stand you."

She headed to the building feeling a little better than she had since getting the news, but trepidation still nipped at her nerves. Normally she handled surprises pretty well, but this had totally caught her off guard.

In a little more than seven months, she was having a baby.

I'm having a baby.

Laz is going to flip.

*

Hours later, Journey dragged herself out of her office and headed to the elevator, exhausted and dealing with a slow-building headache. She had gone back to working extra-long hours and like tonight, was one of the last people to leave the building.

And then there was Laz. She had wimped out and had called him earlier to let him know that something had come up and that she couldn't meet with him tonight. It had been a relief to get his voicemail, but he had called her a couple of times since then, only to get her voicemail. He wasn't the type of man to be ignored, and she already knew that if she didn't call him soon, he'd probably hunt her down.

She pushed the down button for the elevator and leaned against the wall. What she could use was a good night's sleep, something she hadn't gotten since she and Laz agreed to take a break. Now that she thought about it, their separation would've been easier had she officially broken up with him.

But sometime during their shared meals, lounging around chatting, and their steamy nights together, she had fallen in love. Every other thought was of him. Whenever she closed her eyes she saw him, and each time her phone rang, she prayed it was him and hoped it wasn't.

I'm in love with Lazarus Dimas...and I'm having his baby.

Journey's hand went to her stomach. "Unbelievable," she mumbled. Never in a million years had she seen her life going in this direction. Instead of being happy about that realization, she was frustrated. Laz would never change and if she was honest with herself, she didn't want him to; well, at least not totally. He had shaken up her peaceful life, but had also been a bright light in her world. Yes, he was a jerk sometimes, but he was *her* jerk. She even missed their silly arguments as well as the laughs.

I have to talk to him. I have to tell him.

With plans on calling him once she arrived home, she rode the elevator to the ground level, and the moment she stepped off, her cell phone rang. Digging the device out of the side pocket of her handbag, Prentice's name flashed across the screen.

"Hey, Prentice, hold on a sec." She switched over to the Uber app to see if the black car she'd order was close by. *Six minutes.* "Okay, sorry about that. What's up?"

"The murder weapon for the Monsuli case was signed out of evidence three weeks ago."

"By who?"

"Carmen."

"What? Wait, she's been on medical leave since before that time," Journey said, wondering what Carmen had been up to.

"I know, Laz called me and—"

"Prentice, Laz is no longer with the police department. We're done talking to him about this case."

Prentice was quiet for so long, Journey thought that maybe the call had dropped until he spoke.

"Journey, just listen. You can even pretend that you don't hear his name in this conversation, but there's something you should know."

"Fine. What's happened?"

"Someone contacted Carmen a week before the accident and told her that if she didn't make the weapon disappear, they would hurt her ten-year-old daughter."

Journey stood speechless just inside the door that led outside. She thought back on the last time she'd had any interaction with Carmen and could remember Carmen being distracted and anxious. Journey assumed she was struggling with a case.

"Carmen was told that if she went to the police, they'd kill her and her daughter."

"Oh, my God. Is her daughter okay?"

"She's fine. Carmen had immediately sent her to Florida where her uncle lives, and before Carmen could figure out what to do about the threat, the accident happened."

Journey felt sick to her stomach at what her friend must be going through. "That explains why she hasn't returned my calls and why she didn't answer her door when I stopped by yesterday."

"She's terrified, Journey. She finally broke down and contacted Laz this afternoon. He had helped her with an incident with her ex-husband years ago and thought he'd know what to do in this situation. She said that she just hated that she didn't think to call him sooner."

"Where is she now?"

"Laz is taking her to a safe house as we speak. He said he called me since he couldn't reach you."

Laz to the rescue again. He always seemed to be there and know what to do when people needed him.

I should've just answered his call.

His voice message said they needed to talk, but she assumed it was about their relationship, not the case.

"Not sure how Laz did it and he wouldn't tell me, but where he's taking Carmen, she'll be safe. A security firm is providing her personal protection until after the trial."

Journey assumed that he had gotten his new employer involved, which was smart. He'd been pretty sure they'd let him go after the situation with Gabe.

"Oh, and Carmen gave him the knife. He dropped it off to me, and I know you said you wanted the weapon tested again, but Journey, that's going to be useless. It's contaminated with prints."

Journey pinched the bridge of her nose. At this point, the chain of custody was broken and the weapon inadmissible. Besides that, she would never know if Laz had indeed planted the knife…or if Monsuli really did use it as the murder weapon.

"I don't know what to say, Prentice. This case is going to be the death of me. Between witnesses backing out, tainted evidence, threats, people dying…I'm…I'm tired," she said the last part more to herself.

Each case brought its own set of twists and turns, but this one had her on an emotional roller-coaster. She didn't have to ask why because she knew it was mainly due to Laz's involvement.

Journey wanted…no, she *needed* him to be innocent of all wrongdoing, but deep down inside she had a feeling he wasn't. Part of her wanted to know the truth, but there was that other part of her that just wanted it all to go away. Truth be damned.

"I know this has been a tough one for you," Prentice said with sympathy. "But we still have Melody Kane, the ex-mistress's testimony. If we go to trial, her testimony will help."

It might help, but it wouldn't be enough to prove that Monsuli did indeed kill the victim with the knife that they couldn't resubmit into evidence.

Before Journey could respond to Prentice, she glanced outside and saw a black town car stop in front of the door.

"Prentice, I hate to cut this short but my ride is here. I'll call you when I get home. Better yet, let me call you tomorrow when my brain is fresh and I can form some solid questions." Right now, all she wanted to do was go home and go to bed, but first she needed to talk to Laz.

Journey dropped her cell phone into her purse and headed for the car, feeling as if she'd gone through two spin cycles in a washing machine.

"Hi, you're Craig?" she asked the driver when he opened the back door for her, remembering the driver's name and his photo from the Uber app.

"Yes." He smiled and Journey stopped. Alarm bells went off inside her head when she realized he wasn't the same person in the photo.

Something is wrong.

"Oh shoot, Craig. I think I left my files upstairs. I'll be right..." she started, but before she could finish forming her lie, she felt a pinprick on her neck.

"Help!" she screamed before the guy slapped his hand over her mouth.

Panic roared through Journey's body and she wiggled against him, dropping her bag to the ground as she tried to pull away. She couldn't let him put her in the car.

Breaths coming in short spurts, she swung wildly until her fist made contact with his face. He didn't release her, tightening his hold as he lifted her off her feet.

Scared but determined, Journey kicked out her legs and pushed against the inside of the opened door, forcing the guy back until he bumped the car. He loosened his hold, but he didn't let go and she balled her fists and just started moving her arms wildly, hoping to make contact to his body. She didn't care where she hit him as long as she hit him as hard as she could.

"Damn it," he growled, loosening his hold again, giving her just enough slack to make a run for it. But before she could take a step, he reached out and grabbed the back of her blouse, pulling her back.

"Let go! Let me go!" Journey yelled, but she barely heard herself. Something was wrong with her. Something was very wrong as her head grew heavy and her body became weak.

Oh God, my baby. "Wh-what did you in—inject...me..." she started and thought she heard someone call out in the distance.

But a wave of dizziness overpowered her just before her world went black.

Chapter Twenty-Three

Laz paced his living room floor, a two-finger glass of whiskey in his hand and frustration gnawing on his last nerve. He'd been trying to reach Journey for the past couple of hours and she still hadn't returned his call. Even stopping by her condo had proved to be useless.

"This shit is ridiculous." He had honored her wishes of giving her some space, but now that he knew more about what happened with Carmen, the deal was off. Journey might not be safe. Hell, anyone working the Monsuli case might not be safe.

Laz slowed his pacing and sipped the dark liquid, gritting his teeth at the burn slithering down his throat. He had returned an hour ago from getting Carmen settled into a safe house. Mason and Hamilton had really come through, even assigning a security specialist to look after her when Laz explained the situation. Originally, Laz thought that Monsuli might've been behind the threats to Carmen, but now he wasn't so sure. Any number of people could have wanted that knife to disappear, including him.

Laz finished off his drink and set his empty tumbler on the table, his mind on Journey. "Where the hell are you?" he grumbled. She hadn't sounded too good earlier and he'd been looking forward to seeing her, wanting to make sure she was okay. Considering she'd been avoiding him lately, he should've expected her to cancel on him.

His cell phone rang and he shot across the room to retrieve it, only to see *Unknown* on the display. That had been the second call from an unknown number in the past thirty minutes.

Instead of going back to pacing, he sat on the sofa. Two minutes later, when the phone rang again, he answered.

"Yeah."

"Detective Dimas, or should I just refer to you as Mr. Dimas? You're a hard man to reach."

Laz remained silent, trying to place the voice. Only his closest friends and some of his cop buddies had his cell number.

"Who is this?" he finally asked.

"That's not important. What is important is that we have a mutual interest in seeing Enrique Monsuli dead."

Laz froze, his mind racing. "You're going to have to tell me who this is, otherwise this conversation is over."

"See that's the thing. You don't want to hang up on me. From what I've heard, your reach is long and wide. Perfect for making my problem, and your problem of Monsuli's possible release, go away. Trust me, it's in your best interest to see to Monsuli's death."

Unease crept through Laz's veins and he leaned forward. "In my best interest... How so?"

"Well, I have in my possession the beautiful ADA; one who I've heard is important to you. I'll see to her taking her last breath if Monsuli isn't dead within the next twenty-four hours."

Laz's heart stopped. His gut churned with dread as he slowly stood on shaky legs.

There was no way they had snatched Journey. *No way.*

At least that's what he told himself in order to tap down the rage brewing inside him.

"Do we have a deal?"

"Hell no, we don't have a deal!" he snapped, every nerve

in his body wound tighter than the seal on a steel drum. "I want proof of life. Put her on the phone. Now!"

Several excruciating seconds ticked by.

"Laz."

Laz's legs gave out and he dropped to his knees upon hearing her voice. The anguish in that one word had him ready to rip the city apart to find her.

"Journey," he croaked, barely recognizing his own voice. "Are you okay? Did they hurt you?"

"No, but I'm…I'm…" Her voice broke and his heart split in two when she sobbed.

"Aw, baby, don't cry. I'm going to take care of this, and I promise I'm going to find you. Just know that I love you." He heard her soft gasp and another sob. "I love you so damn much."

After a few sniffles, she said, "I love you, too." Her voice sounded a little stronger as if trying to pull herself together. "Please…don't do anything that will—"

"Okay, you talked to her. Now get it done."

Laz leaped up. "Motherfucker, you have just made the biggest mistake of your life! You want to know how far my fucking reach is? Your ass will find out if anything happens to her!"

"Twenty-four hours. You take care of Monsuli and your girl will be released unharmed. It'll be a win-win for both you and me if you make this shit with Monsuli disappear. The only way to do that is if he's dead."

When the line went dead, Laz picked up his empty whisky tumbler and hurled it across the room. "Nooo!" he roared as splinters of glass bounced off the pale wall, raining shards onto the carpet.

How could this have happened?

The full impact of knowing someone had Journey hit him like a two-by-four to the head. His chest tightened and he dropped onto the sofa, desperation clawing through him.

Breathe. Just breathe.

He sat for a few minutes, still feeling as if strong hands

were wrapped around his neck and applying pressure. He needed answers. More importantly, he needed to find Journey.

Think, Laz. Think.

Whoever snatched her knew him. They also probably knew his history with Monsuli, and if they knew he'd been a cop, they had to know the type of shit he could inflict on people who got in his way. And more importantly, they knew he would crawl to the ends of the earth on his hands and knees for Journey.

Twenty-four hours. I have twenty-four hours. I have to find her now.

Heart pounding double time as fear and anger battled within him, Laz rubbed his hands up and down his jean-covered thighs. Hundreds of thoughts bombarded him at once as he tried to decide where to start.

But before he could do anything, he needed to know who he was dealing with.

He quickly dialed one of the tech guys at the station, hoping they could trace the call.

"What's up, man? You miss us yet?"

"Hank, I need your help," Laz said quickly without preamble while he grabbed his weapon, sticking it in the back of his waistband. "Are you at the station?"

"Yeah," he said cautiously.

"Good. I need you to trace my last call."

"Laz, you do realize you don't work here anymore, right? You don't get to—"

"Hank, all I need is for you to trace the call," Laz said with a calm he didn't feel. "That's it. Two minutes and you should be able to pull up what I need."

"Laz, I would if I could," he whispered into the phone. "But we've been given strict instructions not to—"

"It's a matter of life or death. Just do it!"

After a slight hesitation, Hank spoke. "If it's a matter of life or death, then it's a *police* matter. You can't be—"

"Damn it, Hank! I don't have time for this shit. Hell!

Can you trace the call or not?"

"I can't. Ford gave strict orders once you left. No favors. Again, if this is a matter—"

"Fuck it!" Laz yelled into the phone before disconnecting the call. "Damn it!"

Barely holding on to his sanity, he held the phone with both hands in a death grip, willing himself not to throw it across the room. He couldn't think straight. He could barely catch his breath with each inhale and exhale, feeling as if he was suffocating.

I gotta keep it together. I'm no good to her if I lose it.

He went back to pacing. He knew he could get Ashton's help, but he needed someone with tech skills. Someone who could find out who that caller was and someone who could tap into the city's cameras.

He also needed someone to have his back when he hit the streets to search for her.

Hell, he needed a team.

We're a family...we always have each other's back. Malik Lewis's words from weeks ago filtered into Laz's mind. Saying the words and meaning them were two very different things, he thought.

Time to find out if Supreme Security can back up those words.

Since he didn't know how to reach Malik directly, Laz dialed Hamilton's number. The phone rang three times before his friend picked up.

"Hello?" Hamilton answered, his voice thick with sleep.

"Ham..." Laz started, but stopped when a sudden bout of emotion clogged his throat. Fear like he hadn't experienced since losing Gwenn gripped him and squeezed, sucking the calm right out of him.

Laz rubbed his chest, willing himself to speak, but he struggled to get air into his lungs.

"Laz?" When Laz didn't answer, Ham called out his name again, this time with more urgency. "Laz, you there? Talk to me, man."

"Journey..." he swallowed. "Journey's been kid—kidnapped. I need...I need your help."

Chapter Twenty-Four

Laz stood next to Cameron "Wiz" Miller, a computer genius who was part-owner of Supreme Security and was also a former Navy SEAL.

Curious about the guy's background, Laz looked forward to learning more about him, but right now he was just thankful Wiz was willing to help. They, along with Hamilton, Mason and Ashton, were in Wiz's hotel suite watching as he tried hacking into the city's street cameras.

Laz had never felt so helpless in all of his life. He'd been barely able to speak in complete sentences when he called Hamilton. Being paralyzed with fear could do that to a person. But him? He would've never thought it possible, but it wasn't every day you find out that the woman you love more than life has been kidnapped.

"Laz?"

Laz startled when a hand gripped his shoulder. He hadn't even noticed that Hamilton had walked up to him, which let Laz know that he wasn't on his game. Rarely did anyone get a chance to get that close without him knowing.

"Have a seat," Hamilton said, sliding one of the table chairs closer to where Wiz was sitting. "Sit." He pointed to the seat when Laz didn't move.

Laz did as he was told. "I appreciate your help with all of

this," he said to Wiz.

"No prob, man. You're one of us now. This is what we do when our family is in trouble. I'm just glad I was still in town." Wiz talked and typed, his fingers flying across the computer keyboard. He had tried tracing the number of the person who had called Laz, but apparently the guy used an untraceable burner phone. Which none of them was surprised about.

"Yeah, I'm glad, too."

Wiz and a few more people who were a part of Supreme's tech team had been in Atlanta for two days training the IT staff on how to use the company's new intranet.

"One thing you haven't mentioned is what does this person want in exchange for the return of Journey?" Wiz asked over his shoulder.

All eyes were on Laz. He'd told Hamilton about the brief conversation with the caller, and apparently Hamilton hadn't shared it with the others.

"We're going to need to know everything, Laz, in order to help," Ashton said. Laz had been hesitant to pull Ashton into this, not wanting to get him involved in any part that might turn illegal, but now he was glad his friend was there.

Laz didn't know Wiz or Mason all that well, but if Hamilton trusted them, he'd have to also…to a certain extent.

He blew out an exhausted breath and propped his elbow on the table and then rubbed his forehead. He gave them an abbreviated version of the case against Monsuli and how the drug dealer's new lawyers were contesting the verdict.

"What does the caller want from you, Laz?" Mason asked patiently, clearly noticing how Laz had told them everything except answer the original question.

"Let's just say the less you know, the better."

He had twenty-two more hours to find Journey, assuming nothing had happened to her yet. That thought made him sick. Those assholes could be doing anything to her and he was sitting around hoping to get a break into who had taken her.

Silence fell around the room, and even Wiz had stopped typing.

"Trust me, you don't want to know more," Laz continued. "This situation is, um…murky. I will say this, though, I made a promise to Journey that I would walk the straight and narrow. Play everything by the book. I'm not going back on that vow." At least not totally, he thought but didn't say out loud.

"That's good to know," Wiz mumbled while still typing.

Laz had a feeling each guy in the room already knew that he'd break that promise in a heartbeat if necessary. Each of them, at one time or another, had probably made tough calls when it came to keeping their family safe or protecting them.

And there wasn't anything in the world Laz wouldn't do to save Journey.

"I have to find her before it's too late," he mumbled.

Laz ran his hand down his face, fatigue and impatience getting the best of him. It was one o'clock in the morning, two hours since Journey's kidnapper had made his demand.

Sighing, he thought about the quick conversation he'd had with Journey earlier in the day. She had only given him five minutes to speak his piece, but it was then that he had promised to stay on the right side of the law.

I have to keep that promise.

He couldn't dirty his hands by killing Monsuli himself.

Instead, Laz had put in a few calls and cashed in some favors. Actually, he had cashed in a lot of favors, and probably would be indebted to a few people for years to come. All he knew was that he had to find Journey as soon as possible, just in case the situation with Monsuli didn't work out the way the caller requested.

"All right, here…" Wiz said. Laz was out of his seat and standing over the man's shoulder before Wiz could finish his sentence. "Wait. Let me go back to just before the car pulled up to the curb."

Pulse pounding loudly in his ears, Laz and the others watched as the black town car parked on the side of the courthouse. He didn't remember it being so dark on that side of the building and his gaze immediately went to the streetlights. Two were out, yet not the one closest to the car. No way that was a coincidence.

Wiz typed something and the video on the screen showed a little clearer. "According to the time of this video, it looks like they picked her up a couple of hours before contacting you."

Laz cursed under his breath. Why the hell had she still been at work that time of night? He gripped the back of Wiz's chair tighter as he watched Journey stroll out of the building and approached the driver.

"Would be nice if we could hear what she's saying to him," Mason mumbled.

Laz watched intently, wanting to keep his focus on the scene, hoping to spot anything that could help him find her. "She knows somethings not right," he whispered more to himself than to anyone else, watching as she started digging around in her bag. "Good girl. She's stalling. She knows he's not who he's claiming to…"

A needle.

Laz's heart stopped.

Then something inside of him snapped.

"He is a dead man!" he roared and lunged at the computer before thinking.

Wiz stood suddenly, effectively protecting the laptop while the other guys in the room grabbed hold of Laz, barely able to contain him. "He drugged her. That motherfucker drugged her! I am going to *kill* him! I will kill him!"

Breathing hard, he jerked back and forth, struggling to get out of their hold, using everything within him to get them off of him.

"Get the fuck off of me!"

"Not until you calm the hell down!" Ashton ground out, now the only one holding Laz in a bear hug. At 6'4" and two-hundred-and-fifty pounds, he was bigger and stronger.

"Laz, man. You gotta chill. We're going to find her," Hamilton said

"Chill!" Laz thundered, finally shaking Ashton off of him and glaring at his best friend. "You want me to chill? Your ass would be ripping this damn city apart if that was Dakota! Hell, all of you would be tearing up some shit if that were your woman!"

Pulse racing, his gaze went immediately to Wiz. According to Hamilton, Wiz had been through something similar a few years ago with his wife Olivia and her evil twin sister. Laz looked at the other men, knowing they'd be out of their minds and out for blood if either of them had to go through this.

He huffed, his hands covering his face as he struggled to regain his composure. After a few minutes, he dropped his hands and faced the group.

"Just because Journey doesn't carry my last name doesn't mean I wouldn't burn this fucking city down to find her. I *have* to find her."

Wiz was the first one to move when he turned back to his computer and the tension in the room eased up. "I hear you, man," he said. "Let me see if I can tap into any other nearby cameras. Maybe we can get a license plate or something else that can help find this asshole. Oh, and when all of this is over, remind me to tell you about the tracking device I have on my wife."

Laz nodded, still feeling as if a boulder was sitting on his shoulders. He reclaimed his spot over Wiz's shoulder, bracing himself to watch more of the video, feeling more anxious than ever to get answers.

It took everything within him not to lose his shit as he watched her put up a good fight. That helpless feeling that Laz felt earlier slammed into him and his anger was on the brink of exploding again.

He brought his fist to his mouth, trying like hell to stay calm. His other hand, gripping the back of Wiz's chair, tightened as Journey kept fighting before she passed out.

It took Laz a moment to find his words, but then he said, "Is there a way to go back and zoom in on the man? I know he's wearing a cap, but if I can get a better look at his face, neck, anything… Maybe he has a tattoo or some other marks on him that can give me a clue to who he is or who he might run with."

Wiz took several still shots and they all studied the photo. Even with different angles, they didn't get a good look at his face, but then Wiz ran the footage again.

"There!"

"Wait!"

Laz and Ashton yelled at the same time.

"Go back, go back and stop…right there."

"We know him," Ashton said.

"Yeah, that's T-Bone. He used to run with the Disciple Kings," Laz said absently, rubbing the scruff on his chin as he recalled his last dealings with the man's crew. That was the gang Laz had gone after when he found Gwenn dead. Shortly after that, the crew had dismantled, but little by little, some of the members that weren't dead or incarcerated were resurfacing.

With his gaze still on the computer screen, Laz slowly backed away from the guys. "Wiz, you're a lifesaver. I think I can take it from here, though."

"Not without me you're not." Ashton snatched up his jacket and was right behind him.

"Laz," Hamilton dragged out his name, a warning in his tone. "Don't do anything you're going to regret."

"I won't, Ham." Laz was sure his friend knew him well enough to know there wasn't much he regretted, except the rift between him and Journey. But he planned to fix that. "I'm cool. I got this."

"Just make sure your ass doesn't end back up behind bars," Mason added.

Laz nodded. "You got it, boss."

He had no intention of messing up his relationship with

his new team, especially considering how they'd stepped up tonight.

But right now, all Laz could think about was getting Journey back safely while trying to keep at least some of the promises he'd made to her. If he wanted a life with her, he had to start doing everything by the book. At least whenever he could.

He just hoped tonight he could keep his word.

*

"Move and you're a dead man," Laz growled, the muzzle of his 9mm pointed at the side of T-Bone's head.

It was still the middle of the night, and Laz had snuck into his home undetected. Now, with pressure on the back of the T-Bone's neck, he pressed his face into the bed pillow.

"I...can't...breathe." He wiggled, his arms and legs flopping around as he struggled under Laz's hold.

"You don't have to breathe. Just listen," Laz said cryptically. There was just enough moonlight filtering into the room through the side of the blinds for Laz to see the guy's features.

"Get...off me," T-Bone rasped as he tried to move under Laz's weight.

"I will, as soon as you answer my questions. You kidnapped the ADA tonight. Where is she?"

T-Bone froze. If Laz didn't know any better, he would've thought he had also stopped breathing. Scaring him to death was Laz's intention, though he had promised Ashton that he wouldn't kill the man. Considering what Laz had been through tonight, that had been one of the hardest promises to make. What he really wanted to do was snap the guy's neck for even touching Journey, let alone drugging her.

"Where is she?" Laz loosened his hold and the guy lifted his head slightly, gasping for air. When he didn't speak, Laz cocked the gun, pushing it harder against his head. "Start talking. Now!"

"I...I don't know."

"What the fuck do you mean, you don't know? Your ass

is the one who snatched her up."

Laz wasn't a patient man, and he only had a few more minutes to get answers before Ashton and his new partner arrived.

The deal was, when Laz was finished with T-Bone, they'd come in, claiming an anonymous tip of domestic violence and gun shots. Laz had no doubt they'd find drugs and assault weapons on the premises.

"Where. Is. She."

"I don't know!" T-Bone shouted. "Now get off me!"

"Not until you give me more." Laz placed his knee in the guy's back.

"Ow! Get...ow! Okay, okay. I was told to pick her up and park the car in the lot on State Street. I left her in the back seat. I don't know what happened after that."

"What did you drug her with?" The guy didn't respond, only making Laz angrier.

"So help me... What was in the fucking needle?" he seethed. Flashes of the video bombarded Laz's mind and he shook his head, trying to erase the visual on how this man had drugged her.

"I don't know, man! I just did what I was told to do. The needle was in the cup holder." Laz squeezed T-Bone's neck, not bothered by the way he was gagging. "It's...th—the truth."

Laz loosened his hold. "Who gave you the order?"

Again, silence. Laz could smell the man's fear seeping through his pores. When T-Bone didn't respond, Laz grabbed hold of the man's hair and jerked his head back, sticking the gun in his ear.

"Who gave you the damn order?"

"I—I can't... He'll kill me."

"If you don't, I will kill you. Do you hear me? *I. Will. Kill. You.*" Laz had promised to leave the guy alive, but...

"Alonso...Moreno," T-bone said reluctantly, knowing he was a dead man either way. He wasn't even safe in jail.

Alonso Moreno. Monsuli's second-in-command.

"Where can I find him?" Laz finally asked.

"He moves...around. I don't know."

Figuring that was true, Laz eased up. "Okay, so this is what's going to happen. I'm going to leave, but I suggest you keep this visit quiet. If you don't...and if you follow me when I walk out of here, Monsuli will know what you've been doing with his daughter. *His underage* daughter."

"Wh-what? Sh-she's eighteen," T-bone stammered.

"You sure about that?" Laz taunted, knowing the girl was officially an adult, but wanting this jerk to think otherwise.

Laz let that information sink in before he shoved the man's head into the pillow and started to back away. Before he could get to the door, he stopped.

Visions of the way T-Bone had manhandled Journey continued to dominate Laz's mind. He couldn't shake them. All he kept seeing was her trying to fight the man off...and the needle.

T-Bone must have sensed when Laz moved back to the bed. "I told you everything. Just—"

Laz hit him in the back of the head with the butt of his pistol and then left the room. He climbed out of the window that he'd entered through and eased into the back yard. Once he was in the alley, he pulled a burner phone from his pocket and dialed.

"911, what's your emergency?"

"Please send someone quick!" he whispered. "She's screaming and I heard gunshots. Hurry..."

Laz gave them the address, but when they asked for his name, he said John Doe and then faded into the darkness.

Chapter Twenty-Five

Journey jerked awake and tensed when a piercing pain shot from the top of her head to the base of her neck. Blinking several times, she tried pushing away the sleep still clogging her mind, but struggled to keep her eyes open.

The room was dark with just a hint of light coming from somewhere, but not enough for her to see anything. Fear had been her companion earlier but screaming for help hadn't accomplished anything but hoarseness and a sore throat.

I'm so tired...and hungry. At least they'd given her bottled water, but she felt so weak.

"Help! Please. Help me!" she yelled, but barely heard her own voice as defeat tried to consume her. *I'm not giving up. I can't give up,* she thought to herself.

She wiggled and rocked as much as she could in the hard wood chair, hoping to loosen the constraints on her wrists. Not only were her hands bound behind her back, but her ankles were tied with rope around the leg of the chair. Every muscle in her body ached, but whenever she was dozing off, she tried to keep moving, tried to stay hopeful that Laz would find her.

I love you. I love you so damn much.

His words floated through her mind on a continuous loop. She knew she had fallen in love, but she never thought she'd hear those words from him. Now he might be risking his freedom and his life...for her.

The people who kidnapped her promised not to hurt her as long as Laz saw to Monsuli's death. There was no way he could do what they asked of him without ramifications. She could admit to wanting the whole Monsuli case to go away, but not like this.

Not at the risk of losing Laz.

Tears filled her eyes and regret assailed her as she thought about the baby. She should've told him about the baby the moment she found out, but instead she let fear and selfishness keep her from talking to him. And for what? It all seemed so silly now.

At least she'd gotten a chance to tell him that she loved him.

A sudden chill filled the air, and Journey shivered, coldness seeping deeper into her bones. She had worn pants to work which offered some coverage on her legs, but the thin blouse was doing nothing to ward off the cold.

I have to get out of here. She had no idea where she was or who the kidnappers were since they kept their faces covered even when they let her talk to Laz.

He's going to find me. Journey knew that he was probably searching every inch of the city for her, but she couldn't just sit around and wait. She had to figure out a way to...

Journey startled when the lights popped on. Squinting, her eyes were slow to adjust to the poor lighting, but she took in the room. Small with gray concrete floors and walls, and no windows. She'd been in a haze when they put her in the room, but she would have remembered the flat screen television sitting on a roll-away stand several feet in front of her now.

Journey gasped when the television suddenly came on and Monsuli's face filled the screen. Her heart beat faster as the words "breaking news" scrolled beneath the photo before the reporter appeared on the screen.

In breaking news, overnight...

Overnight, Journey thought. Exactly how long had she been there?

As we mentioned earlier, notable drug lord Enrique Monsuli was found dead in his cell early this morning. The guards on duty discovered him hanging from his bedsheets. Early reports are saying that he committed suicide. So far there has been no evidence of foul play. We'll keep you informed of any new developments throughout the day.

Journey's mouth dropped open.

Oh. My. God.

How was that possible? Shock and fear battled within her. No way a man who was appealing his murder case would commit suicide. But the alternative…

"I guess it's true what I've heard about Detective Dimas."

Journey jumped at the sound of her captor's voice, awe in his tone. He spoke with an accent, but she couldn't tell its origin. She also couldn't see him since he was standing somewhere behind her.

"Oops, I should've said Lazarus Dimas. I forget. He's no longer a cop, which still surprises me, but somehow I bet you had something to do with that decision, too."

Anger bubbled inside Journey as she ignored this guy's last comment. All she could think about was Monsuli and Laz's possible involvement in his death. No way would Laz risk going to jail for murder, even for her.

Yes he would, a small voice inside her head whispered. *'I'm also very protective."* His words from when they talked about dating slammed into her memory. She prayed he had nothing to do with this, but deep down she knew.

"Just let me go. You got what you wanted."

"Rumor has it," he said as if she hadn't spoken, "when motivated, Dimas is vigilant when it comes to righting a wrong and protecting those he loves."

"Then you should know by kidnapping me, you've put a target on your head." The words were out of her mouth without thinking. This guy had promised not to hurt her and she wanted to keep it that way. But Journey hated knowing that he might have forced Laz to do something he wouldn't have done otherwise. "You got what you want. Now let me go," she demanded with more bravado than she felt.

The man chuckled, but even twisting back and forth in her chair, she couldn't see him. "Attorney Ramsey, I would think you'd be happy to have one less case to handle. Prison was too good for Monsuli. As for Dimas coming after me, he'd have to find me first."

She almost told him that Laz would definitely find him, but she kept her mouth closed. She wanted all of this to be over with once and for all. "Just let me go."

"I'll let your boyfriend know where you are. It'll be up to him to come and get you, but I'll be long gone by then."

"Please...please if you're not going to let me go yet, can you at least untie me? The ropes are too tight. They're cutting off my circulation. I promise, I won't try to get away," Journey lied. If she got a hint of an opportunity to get out that place, she was taking it. She hated feeling so helpless, waiting around for someone to rescue her. For as long as she could remember, she always took care of herself and rarely had to depend on others.

"Nice try, but I can't do that."

Before Journey could form her next thought, the television went out and the room went black.

"No...no! Don't leave me! Let me go!" she screamed, rocking back and forth in the chair. With what little strength she had, Journey jerked against the ropes, not caring about the pain shooting through her arms and legs as she tried to break free.

I have to get out of here.

Tears flooded her eyes as she continued wrestling with the restraints, her efforts proving fruitless.

"Sit still before you hurt yourself," the same voice said, startling her. She thought he had left the room. "I assured Dimas that you'd be unharmed, and I try to always keep my word. Though I hate to leave you here alone, our time together has come to an end. I'll make sure you're comfortable before I leave."

Journey jerked when she felt a pinprick in her neck and she cried outright. She had asked earlier what he had drugged her with, but he only laughed.

God...please let my baby be okay.

A short while later, her body grew heavy like before. Despite the efforts to keep her eyes open, she succumbed to the sleep that pulled her under.

*

"I guess asking if you're okay would be a dumb question," Hamilton said.

Laz stared out the passenger side window of Hamilton's truck, still feeling as if someone had a tight grip around his neck. From the moment he received the call, he had been on adrenaline overload and couldn't remember the last time he'd eaten or slept.

"I don't know if I'll ever be okay. All I keep thinking about is those assholes having Journey in some damn warehouse. Do you know how much shit I've done in warehouses?"

"No, but I can imagine."

The warehouse images of his past rushed back to him like a bullet to the chest. How many times had he taking a perp to one in order to scare some sense into them? Or the number of times he'd been under cover and met in a warehouse. Or most recently, the time he knocked Scott around a little for the hurting he had put on elderly people. If any of those scenarios played out with those who took Journey, Laz didn't know what he would do.

"If they hurt her I—"

"Don't go there, man. She's fine."

Hamilton exited off the highway in Alpharetta and Laz's anxiety increased as they followed the navigation system's directions. He pulled on the collar of the long-sleeved T-shirt he was wearing, suddenly finding it hard to breathe. It was barely daybreak and despite the fifty-five-degree morning, he lowered the window.

"Just sit tight. We should be there in a few minutes. He assured you she was fine."

He being Alonso Moreno.

Moreno didn't know that Laz knew his identity, but he'd soon find out. He might not have been the one to shove Journey into the car, but based on additional information beside T-Bone's admission, Moreno had orchestrated the snatch.

The guy had definitely done his homework, but little did he know, so had Laz. It was only a matter of time before Moreno suffered the same fate as Monsuli.

Laz thought about the call he'd gotten from his contact at the prison a couple of hours ago. It worked to Laz's benefit that Monsuli had more enemies than friends. All Laz had to do was make the right connections to get the job done without actually taking out Monsuli himself. At the time, he hadn't asked or wanted to know how the task would be done. He had just hoped it could be done.

Suicide.

Laz hadn't seen that one coming. There was a little guilt nipping at his nerves, but mostly what he was feeling was anxiety and a desperation to find Journey and make sure she was okay.

He sat up straighter when they pulled into an empty parking lot of an abandoned warehouse.

"Go around to the back and park by the door on the end." Forty-five minutes ago, he had been given instructions on exactly where to find her.

Laz just hoped…

The moment Hamilton slowed, Laz was out of the truck before the vehicle came to a complete stop. With his gun and flashlight in his hands, he pulled open the heavy metal door that led into the semi-dark musty building. Anger and fear warred within him, unsure of what he'd find.

She has to be okay.

It was colder in there than it was outside, and the musty odor made him almost positive there was mold and mildew in the place. He had only been there a few minutes and already he struggled to breathe. His concern for Journey surged. There were a few windows, most riddled with holes the size of large rocks, but none provided much ventilation.

"Those bastards left her in this shit hole," Laz muttered, then coughed as dust from the dirt floor kicked up with each step he took. He moved around old steel plates, debris and a host of other shit he couldn't identify at the moment. "Journey!"

"Calm down, Laz," Hamilton said when he caught up to him. "If you're freaked out when you find her, she's going to freak out."

"I can't calm down," Laz growled, checking each small room they passed, making sure they were empty. He swallowed hard, trying to manage the impatience that was making him want to tear the place apart. When he neared the second-to-the-last door—the room they said she'd be in— Laz struggled to calm his pounding heart.

He stopped in the doorway and his temper flared. "They fucking tied her up!"

Journey was on the other side of the room lying on a filthy sofa, her back to the door. His rage mounted. The room, semi-dark, damp, and nasty, only made him angrier.

She's not moving.

Panic rioted within him, and then dread lodged in his gut when he saw the needle on the floor next to her.

"No," he choked out, feeling as if someone had reached into his chest and grabbed hold of his heart and squeezed. "God, no."

Not again.

He hadn't realized he had stopped in the middle of the floor until Hamilton moved past him, hurrying to her side. "She's alive," he said after turning her over, his fingers against her neck. "Her pulse is strong, but she's freezing." Hamilton started shaking out of his lightweight jacket.

Laz shoved him out of the way and made quick work of untying her hands and feet. "Journey. Journey," he choked out, barely able to hold himself together. He made note of the vicious-looking rope burns and the areas of broken skin on her wrists and ankles. He wasn't a praying man, but he sent up a silent prayer hoping she was okay. She had to be okay.

"Put this around her," Hamilton said, handing over his jacket.

Laz wrapped it around her. "Journey. Sweetheart, come on, wake up."

He shook her several times, gently tapping her cheek as he continued calling her name. His mind was a crazy mixture of rage and fear as he cradled her against him.

"Come on. I need you to open those gorgeous eyes."

She moaned.

Laz hadn't cried since he lost Gwenn, but damned if his eyes didn't fill with tears. Blinking rapidly, he quickly swiped them away before they could fall as he got his emotions under control.

It was still a while before her eyes eased open and she blinked several times, as if trying to focus.

"No. Don't touch me," she said in a hoarse whisper as she fought him, trying to get away. Her weakness was evident in the way she could barely lift her arms.

"Journey, it's me. It's Laz," he said quietly while she still struggled to wake completely. "Come on, baby, I need you to wake up."

"Laz," she rasped and sagged against him, fisting the front of his shirt. She was mumbling something, but he couldn't understand a word through her sobs.

"I've got you," he said into her hair. He held her close, probably tighter than he should, but he couldn't help it. It had been a long time since he'd been this scared, and it seemed like forever since he'd held her in his arms. "I love you so damn much. I thought I had lost you." His voice was rough with emotion as he struggled to keep himself together.

Hamilton gripped his shoulder. "Laz, we need to get out of here and get her checked out."

He was right, but Laz didn't know if he would ever be able to let her go again. He eventually loosened his hold and kissed her.

"Are you hurt anywhere?" he asked not sure she'd be able to answer him.

"My head.... It was dark. They...they left me." Tears poured out of her eyes and it felt as if someone was stabbing him in the heart over and over again.

"I know, baby, and I will make them pay."

She started shaking her head, but winced and fell into him. "No more," she pleaded, her voice so weak and raspy, Laz could hardly understand her. "Promise...no fi—fighting. Please..."

"Okay, okay. I promise." He wiped her face, unable to keep up with the tears flowing freely. So far, his promises to her had been good for shit, and this would be yet another promise he wouldn't be able to keep. Especially seeing her like this.

"Don't feel good," Journey mumbled, her hand going to her stomach and she moaned as she curled deeper into him.

"Are you going to be sick?" Laz asked in a rush. He wasn't letting her go.

She didn't say anything, just kept holding her stomach and moaning. What had they done to her?

"Come on. Let's get out of here," Hamilton said, grabbing the flashlight Laz had abandoned and shining it toward the floor to guide their way back out of the building.

Laz stood with Journey in his arms, holding her close as they hurried toward the exit. Worry consumed him. She was so light in his arms, much lighter than the last time he'd carried her.

The weight loss wasn't something that happened overnight. No. Clearly, she hadn't been eating and taking care of herself.

"Laz," she moaned.

"I got you, sweetheart." He kept moving, hoping that nothing was seriously wrong with her as she curled deeper into him, crying softly as she held her stomach.

"Our baby...help...the baby."

Laz stopped in his tracks. "Wait... What?"

No way had she just said what he thought he'd heard. Yet, one look at Hamilton, who stood less than a foot away with raised eyebrows, and Laz knew he hadn't heard wrong.

"Journey," he croaked around the lump in his throat, unable to move and scared to death when she passed out in his arms. "Journey, what are you saying? Talk to me. Come on, sweetheart." He gently shook her, but she was out.

"We gotta move. Now!" Hamilton said in a rush and took off in a jog with Laz hot on his heels.

A baby?

Chapter Twenty-Six

Laz stood in the doorway of Journey's bedroom, staring at her as she slept. In the last couple of days, he had experienced every emotion known to mankind. From fear to rage, from panic to relief, from shock to elation, all of them more intense than the next.

And all of them centered around the woman he couldn't see living without.

I'm going to be a father.

The thought seemed so foreign. Each time the words filtered into his brain, Laz shook his head, struggling to grasp the idea. He had often thought about marriage and having a family, but to have it become a reality was more than he could've hoped for. He didn't have the marriage part of the dream, yet, but one day... One day soon he had every intention of asking Journey to become his wife.

She stirred and Laz moved across the room to the bed. Sitting on the edge of it next to her, he ran the back of his fingers down her soft cheek. He wasn't trying to wake her, but with what they'd just been through, he needed to touch her. Needed to be close to her.

When she moaned with her eyes still closed and rested her hand on her stomach, Laz immediately went on alert. He didn't know how he was going to survive seven months of her being pregnant without him freaking out. With every wince, moan, sigh, or move she made, he wanted to know if she was okay, if she was in pain, or if she needed anything.

"Laz."

"I'm right here." She'd been sleeping a lot, which was expected with all things considered, and she hadn't said much, claiming she didn't feel like talking. But each day, she was growing stronger and more talkative. Soon she'd be back to normal. At least he hoped.

Journey didn't open her eyes right away, but eventually turned her head slightly and looked at him through half-lifted lids.

"Do you need something?" he asked.

"Only you."

That brought a smile to his face. Every nerve in his body had been on high alert from the moment she had mentioned *the baby* at the warehouse. A small part of him thought that maybe she'd been delusional, while the other part of him had been scared to death that she might've been pregnant and those assholes had endangered her and his child.

Stripping down to his boxer briefs, Laz climbed into the bed and pulled her against the side of his body, loving how she curled into him. "Do you feel okay?"

"Still a little tired, but I feel better than I have in a while." She snuggled closer. "I'm just glad to be home...with you."

"Me too, baby."

If Laz thought he'd been scared crazy when he first received the call from the kidnapper, it was nothing compared to what he experienced on the ride to the hospital. He could honestly say he had never been that afraid in all of his life.

That fear had multiplied when he waited for the hospital staff to run tests on Journey, including a pregnancy test. The toxicology report had come back stating she'd had a low amount of temazepam, a sleep aid, in her system. It was too early in the pregnancy to know if it had any effect on the baby, but the doctor was optimistic.

The handful of people who knew about the abduction had agreed to keep it quiet, including Geneva, who Laz had called once he got to the hospital. Geneva had taken the news better than expected, and agreed to notify her parents, who had been scheduled to return from an overseas trip the next day.

So far, neither the media or the DA's office had gotten wind of anything. Wiz had worked his magic and somehow erased the footage of Journey's abduction outside of the courthouse, while Laz had told the hospital staff that he had found Journey unresponsive at her apartment.

Once she was coherent, he'd had a chance to fill her in on the story they'd decided to go with.

"Hopefully my parents didn't drive you crazy. I would've preferred you meet them under different circumstances."

Laz smiled. "Yeah, me too. I thought for sure when your father found out you were pregnant that he was going to shoot me. I'm ninety-nine percent sure he was packing."

Laz felt Journey smile against his chest. "My dad wouldn't have shot you, but you're probably right about him carrying a weapon. Like you, he doesn't go too many places without one. Also like you, as a former cop, he's still very intimidating. He used to be the master at scaring away boyfriends."

Laz laughed, thinking he would be the same way with his daughters. "Do you think you'll ever tell them about the kidnapping?" he asked. The subject was still touchy for her and she hadn't wanted to talk about the incident any more than necessary.

"No."

"Well, just so you know, I think your father suspects we were holding something back from them."

Journey lifted her head, her troubled eyes meeting his. "Why do you say that?"

"When he and I went to the living room after leaving you and your mother in here, he bombarded me with questions. Despite your long-sleeved shirt, he saw the bruises on your wrists. He also said that you wouldn't put your unborn child at risk by taking any type of medication. And then he asked me point blank—*What aren't you and Journey telling us?*"

"Oh no." She brought her hand to her mouth. "What did you tell him?"

"I told him that there was an incident with a few bad guys, but the situation had been handled and was being kept quiet."

"You two are a lot alike. It's almost scary. I'm sure that response wasn't enough for him."

"Nope, it wasn't." Laz recalled the stare-down and the lethal glare brewing in her father's eyes. "He had more questions, but when he realized that I wasn't going to share more, he told me that my reputation precedes me. And he hoped I had handled anyone that had hurt you."

"Oh, Lord."

Laz laughed. "Yeah, it seems when your father found out we were dating, he did some digging into my background."

Journey shook her head and sighed. "Yeah, I bet he did. Me and Geneva could never get away with anything, though my sister tried."

Laz had no doubt about that. Geneva was a sneaky one.

"Your dad still has some connections at Atlanta PD from when he was a cop, and he told me that some of what he heard about me was disturbing. He also said a lot of other things," Laz shrugged, "but I'll keep that between him and I. But I reiterated that the situation had been dealt with and assured him that he didn't have to worry about you. I made it clear that going forward, I would do whatever necessary to make sure you and our baby are well taken care of and safe."

Searching his eyes, Journey studied him for the longest time without speaking. It was only a matter of time before she asked if he did anything to the people responsible for the kidnapping. But she knew him well enough to know that he wouldn't be volunteering any information, and even if she did question him, his answers would be vague.

Laz had a feeling she either didn't want to know or wasn't ready to talk about the events leading up to her kidnapping or those that followed. Except for when she had talked to the DA the day before, acknowledging that she had heard about Monsuli's suicide, she hadn't mentioned the case or anything related to it to Laz.

She laid her head back down on his chest. "I know I've said this before, but thanks for coming for me," she said quietly.

"I would walk through fire for you. You have to know that. Whether you're pissed at me and giving me the silent treatment or not, Journey, there is *nothing* I wouldn't do for you...and our baby." And he meant what he told her father. He would ensure Journey and the baby's safety, but revenge dominated his thoughts.

Laz hadn't been able to pull himself away from Journey's side while at the hospital, but that didn't stop him from calling in a couple of more favors to the underworld. He had even offered a reward for anyone who found Moreno. It was only a matter of time.

"I'm glad you're excited about the baby," Journey whispered. "I just wish I would've told you the moment I suspected I was pregnant."

"All that matters is that I know now." It was probably good he hadn't known. He had already been a wreck with her missing. Knowing she was pregnant and missing would've probably sent him over the edge.

During her short stay in the hospital, Geneva had filled Laz in on the day Journey had officially found out she was pregnant. He was a little surprised to hear about her insecurities regarding becoming a mother, but tried to understand where she was coming from. He had already known that she had no intention of getting married and having kids, although he had hoped to one day change her mind. Up until now, building her career had been her sole focus.

After the doctor had ran a series of tests, she had broken down in tears, fearing the baby wouldn't be okay. She faulted herself for everything, including getting pregnant in the first place. Laz had tried reassuring her that even if she had missed a few days from taking the pill, both of them were responsible for birth control. No way was he letting her take the blame.

Once she started feeling better physically, it seemed to help her emotionally. Now she seemed excited about their new addition, especially knowing that he was thrilled about becoming a father. Sure, the prospect of parenthood was scary as hell, but Laz looked forward to the challenge. Even more so knowing they'd be raising the baby together.

"I understand why you didn't tell me right away," Laz said. "But going forward, let's agree that we do a better job communicating. If something or someone is bothering you, I want to know. If you're unhappy or hurting or anything else, I want to know."

After a slight hesitation, she said, "I'll only agree if that works both ways."

Laz knew he wasn't the best communicator, but if he wanted this relationship to work, there were a number of changes he had to make.

"Agreed."

Chapter Twenty-Seven

Three days later

No more fighting. No more breaking the law. No more hanging out in jail, Laz. Promise me.

Journey's plea from the day before taunted Laz as he added the chopped vegetables to the egg mixture for her omelet. They'd spent the day before binge-watching a law enforcement show on television and Journey had compared him to one of the main characters. A character who took shit from no one and bent the rules in half during most episodes.

Laz found the show entertaining and actually liked the guy. He didn't see any problem with the way the man operated, getting the job done no matter what. But Journey, on the other hand, had cringed during most of his scenes. And of course Laz had to hear about it.

Then she made him promise her that he was done with that life. A life that skated on the edge of justice.

I hate making promises.

All night, her words and the pleading in her eyes had clogged his mind. When he wasn't thinking about that, he was reliving the moment he found her in the warehouse. The rope burns. Her lifeless body. The needle. He didn't know if he would ever be able to let go of those images.

"Yeah, I'll keep my promise. Right after this one last job," he whispered and slid the omelet onto a plate. Alonso Moreno would regret the day he ever laid a hand on her.

It was only a matter of time.

Laz organized the omelet, sausage, hash browns, and orange juice onto the breakfast tray. He put the waffles on a different plate and set it near the tray while he made Journey a cup of tea.

"All right. I think that's it," he said to himself, double-checking to make sure he had everything.

His cell phone, sitting on the breakfast bar, rang right after he added the tea cup to the tray. Laz snatched up the phone, hoping it was the call he'd been waiting days for.

"Yeah."

"It's done," the caller said. Laz recognized the voice immediately. Before the other day, he hadn't spoken to this contact since the night he called him about roughing up Gabe.

"Are you sure?" Laz questioned. The boulder-like weight that had been sitting on his chest since finding out Journey had been kidnapped was finally crumbling away.

"Positive. You'll never have another problem out of Alonso Moreno. May he rest in peace."

Or not.

After being filled in on the details, Laz said, "I'll take care of tipping off Atlanta PD." He disconnected and set the phone back on the counter, glad that he had taken care of all of the loose ends.

It is done. Finally.

*

Journey awaken slowly, stretching her arms up and out as she released a noisy yawn. Though still a little achy, for the most part, she was starting to feel like herself. No doubt the way Laz and Geneva had been practically pouring water down her throat and force-feeding her had helped.

She glanced to her right, not surprised to find the space on the other side of the bed empty. Laz was one of those irritating morning people. It didn't matter what time he went to bed, he was usually up before dawn.

Journey headed to the bathroom, freshened up, and then pulled one of Laz's T-shirts from the closet, but stopped in front of the full-length mirror. With the shirt thrown over one shoulder, she placed her hands on her stomach, still in awe that a baby was growing inside of her. It would be a couple of months before she really started showing, and a part of her was looking forward to seeing the transformation of her body.

No longer afraid, she couldn't wait to meet their baby.

A wistful sigh slipped through her lips as she put on the T-shirt. Laz hadn't officially moved in with her, but hadn't left her side for any long period of time since their ordeal. The kidnapping had definitely brought them closer, but she didn't know if she would ever fully recover mentally. She had never been through anything that scary in all of her life.

Journey moved back into the bedroom and had started making the bed when the door swung open.

"Oh, good. You're awake." Laz walked into the room with a tray loaded with food.

"Wow, what's all that?"

"How about breakfast in bed?"

"Mmm, it looks and smells so good." She threw the covers back and climbed into the bed. As she spied the omelet, sausage and hash browns, her mouth watered in anticipation. "I'm suddenly starving."

Laz set the tray across her lap, and after fluffing two pillows for his back, he positioned himself next to her on the bed.

"This is so thoughtful. Thank you," Journey said, taking a big gulp of the juice.

"Anything for you, babe."

Hungry, Journey cut a piece of the sausage patty and brought it to her mouth, but stopped. "Ugh," she groaned, her stomach suddenly queasy at the smell of the meat. She covered her mouth with her hand and set the fork down, hoping the feeling would pass.

"What?" Laz asked, and quickly moved the tray from over her legs. "What is it?"

"The sausage…the smell." So far, she hadn't fallen prey to morning sickness, but she had noticed some smells made her nauseous. Apparently, sausage was one of them.

"No sausages. Check."

Laz handed her the cup of tea, took the sausage patties off the plate, and put them into one of the napkins. The day before, they found out hot wings was another item she wouldn't be having for a while.

"Anything else I should take away?"

Journey took several sips of the hot tea, slowly feeling better, and shook her head. She hoped he didn't have to take anything else away because she really was hungry, and couldn't wait to eat the hash browns.

Before repositioning the tray, Laz rubbed his large hand over her stomach in a soothing manner, and Journey's heart fluttered. Sometimes his tenderness caught her off guard. Like now, when he placed a kiss where his hand had just been. She was so glad he was excited about the baby, and hadn't been angry about her keeping the news from him.

"I love you so much," he said, and a smile tugged on the corner of her lips.

"And I love you…more than I'll ever be able to express."

As he'd done at the start of every morning they'd been together, Laz pulled her close for a lingering kiss.

"You taste sweet," Journey said, licking her lips.

He snapped his fingers. "Shoot. That reminds me. I forgot your waffles. Be right back."

Journey dug into the meal. Laz had been catering to her every need and want, but tomorrow they'd have to go back to reality. She had taken some much-needed time off from the office, and Laz would be starting another assignment with Supreme Security. She was so glad he was no longer a cop, but knew that security work brought its own set of danger.

"Here you go." He added the waffles to the limited space on the tray.

"If you keep this up, you're going to spoil me." She fed him some of the omelet and then gathered another forkful for herself, moaning her appreciation of how good it tasted. The man was not only *fine*, but he could cook, too.

"That's the least I can do. I'm still working to get back into your good graces."

"Laz, we already talked about this. Clean slate. I know it's easier said than done, but I want us to start fresh. We have to try and forget about the mistakes we've made and the choices..." Her voice trailed off as she thought about how she had blackmailed Gabe, and the way she'd mishandled parts of the Monsuli case.

During that visit she'd had with Gabe in his hospital room, he had signed the document she had drawn up, agreeing to her terms regarding the charges against Laz. He had also given his resignation the day after being released from the hospital. So far, he had done everything she requested. He had even followed through and entered a drug treatment center in San Antonio.

"Hey," Laz said, his hand massaging the back of her neck. "No regrets. We both have done what we felt we needed to do. Clean slate."

Journey nodded and continued eating, feeding Laz in between bites.

The last few months had been like a dream in some ways and a nightmare in others. Since the kidnapping, she didn't know if she would ever be able to be in a completely dark room again. Now that she knew she'd been left in an abandoned warehouse that had rodents, spiders, and God knew what else, she was glad she had slept through most of the ordeal.

She lifted her fork, loaded with hash browns. "Want some more?"

"Nah, I'm good." Laz leaned back against the headboard, his penetrating gaze steady on her.

She ate a few more bites before moving the tray off to the side. "What are you thinking about?"

"How much I love you, and how that scares the hell out of me."

She narrowed her eyes. "I love you too, honey, but it doesn't scare me. Why does it scare you?"

He pulled her against his side and kissed the top of her head. "I can't begin to explain the fear that tore through my body when we found you unresponsive. And then to find out you went through all of that carrying my baby…"

She didn't remember much about those first few minutes after he found her, unsure if some parts were real or if she had still been half-asleep. What she did remember, though, was seeing Laz more vulnerable than she had ever seen him.

"I have been shot, shot at, and have witnessed some gruesome acts of violence. Shit you would never believe."

Journey shivered against him, just thinking about what a cop's job entailed.

"None of that…" He swallowed, wiping his hand over his mouth. "None of that prepared me for seeing your unmoving body and that needle. You are such a part of me, Journey, I felt as if…as if I was going to die."

Laz had told her when he first saw the needle, it was as if he'd been reliving a nightmare. He insisted Journey's kidnappers knew about Gwenn, and their intent to taunt Laz mentally and emotionally with the needle had hit its mark. He'd said that every time he closed his eyes, he saw both her and Gwenn with needles lying beside them.

"Were you serious about not going after Alonso Moreno and his people?"

Laz moved his arm from around her and banged his head against the headboard. "Journey, you've asked me that every day. I told you I'm done with all of that unless they do anything else to disrupt our lives. I know I still have to earn your trust, and from this day forward I will always keep my word to you."

Journey trusted him…for the most part. She still

wondered about his role in Gabe's first beating, and then there was the knife. She might never know if he actually planted evidence, but...

She turned to her side to better look at Laz. "If I ask you a question, will you answer me honestly?"

He stared at her in that way he often did, as if looking deep into her soul.

"For now on, I will answer any and all of your questions honestly. But are you sure you can handle my answers? Journey, I've done some things recently and in my past that would probably have you running to another country. Don't ask me anything unless you know you can handle the answer."

Well, all righty then.

"Um...that's all right. I guess I don't need to know." She was curious by nature, but might never know the answers to those particular questions. That was okay since she planned to never look back.

"Now, I have a question for you."

She looked at him warily. "Ooo-kay."

"Did you have anything to do with Hall dropping the charges against me, and then resigning and leaving town?"

Of all the questions he could've asked, that wasn't one she was expecting.

"Well...ask me no questions, and I'll tell you no lies."

A slow smile spread across his enticing lips, and he burst out laughing.

"Well damn, counselor. I guess I'm not the only one in this relationship who plays hardball. Okay, you don't have to answer, but let's say that you did have something to do with how that all played out. I would have loved to hear that conversation. If you were as kickass as you usually are in court, Hall didn't stand a chance. You, my dear are definitely the queen of getting what you want."

Journey smiled. "Yeah and I'm afraid that over the past few months, you might have rubbed off on me."

"Good to know," he said, smiling before he turned

serious. "I can guarantee you this."

"What's that?"

She squealed when he flipped her onto her back and hovered above her. "Our relationship will never be boring."

"Oh?" She traced his lips with her finger. "And how are you going to guarantee that?"

"Well, I can show you better than I can tell you."

"In that case, show me, baby."

He flashed that sexy grin that made her immediately wet and used his knees to spread her legs. "Oh, I plan to."

When Laz lowered his head and his lips touched hers, heat soared to the center of Journey's core. Her body always responded to him immediately; she would never tire of the way he turned her on with little or no effort. A kiss here. A touch there. Even the way he gazed into her eyes made her horny and wet.

But now, when he kissed her, caressing her lips with his, she could feel his love pouring from him. Never in a million years did she think she could feel like this, her heart so full of love for this man. She didn't know what the future held for them. All she knew was that she would never take another day with him for granted.

When Laz covered her body with his, her eager response had her reaching for the snap on his jeans, but then he stopped moving.

"Damn it." He lifted up and started to move from the bed, but Journey held on to his waistband.

"What's wrong?"

"I need to go get something."

"Now?" she shrieked, shocked that he was leaving the bed just as things were heating up. "Laz!"

He grinned and gave her a quick kiss. "Get naked. I'll be right back."

Journey hurried out of the T-shirt and her panties and tossed them on the floor next to the bed. She was pulling the sheet over herself when Laz returned.

"Out of your clothes, detective. I mean… Man, I'm

going to have to find a new nickname for you."

Laz laughed and climbed onto the bed without shedding his T-shirt and jeans.

Journey narrowed her eyes at him. "What are you up to? One minute you're kissing and filling me up, the next—"

"Will you marry me?" he asked and seemed to pull a diamond ring out of thin air. Journey sat stunned, her mouth hanging open. "I know we haven't talked about marriage in great detail, and I know you think marriage is a dirty word. But if I promise to love you unconditionally, and make sure your life with me is fun, exciting, and full of amazing sex, will you marry me?"

Journey's eyes filled with tears and her hands covered her mouth as she stared at the man who had already made her life anything but boring.

There had been a time when she hadn't planned on ever getting married, but since Laz came into her life, she found herself doing a lot of things she thought she'd never do.

"Well?" he questioned, suddenly looking a little unsure, which was not a look she usually saw on him. "Do you wanna be my wife?"

Journey laughed and then nodded. "Yeah. Yeah, I'd love to be your wife."

Epilogue

Four months later...

"Who the hell ever heard of a gender reveal party?" Laz grumbled as they stood in front of a long table that was still loaded with food and drinks even after most of their guests had eaten. On the wall behind the table was a banner that read: *Basketball or Ballet?* Pink and blue balloons were attached to the ends of the food table, as well as the small dessert table next to it.

"Watch your language. You know Dom is good at popping up when you least expect," Journey said, glancing around the first floor of her sister's home where their guests were eating, talking and laughing. "As for the party, you weren't complaining when you filled your second plate of food."

Laz slid his arms around her growing waist and pulled her to his side, placing a kiss on her temple. "True, but I still don't see the point of all of this. And what do the cupcakes have to do with anything?"

In the center of the small dessert table, there were tons of cupcakes decorated with pink and blue frosting.

"Those are the *reveal* cupcakes. We'll know what we're having once we bite into them. Pink filling means we're having a girl. If the filling is blue, we're having a boy."

Laz shook his head still not seeing the point. They could've just allowed the doctor to tell them. During their last ultrasound, the obstetrician had asked if they wanted to know the sex of the baby. They both wanted to know, but Journey didn't want to know at that moment. She explained that Dakota had suggested they do a gender reveal party, and Journey's sister, Geneva, offered to host it. Supposedly, the only people who knew the gender of their baby were those at the bakery.

Laz turned Journey into his arms so she could face him. "Since your sister won't let us eat the cupcakes yet, how about you and I go upstairs and pick a bedroom to hang out in." He nuzzled her neck, enjoying the way she squirmed against him. "I have a few new moves that I'd love to show you."

Journey laughed. "Mmhm, I bet you do." She wrapped her arms around him, running her fingers through his hair. He loved the feel of her hands in his hair, but he loved it even more whenever she kissed him, the way she was doing now.

The last few months had been a whirlwind of activity and Laz couldn't ever remember being this happy. He worked full-time for Supreme Security, and had he known the job would be so rewarding, Laz would've left Atlanta PD years ago. As for Journey, her work life went back to normal, except her work hours weren't as long. Monsuli's death had been officially ruled a suicide, and Laz was relieved when the judge vacated the conviction, and the case had been closed.

"All right, Mr. and Mrs. Dimas, keep the PDA to a minimum," Geneva mumbled, shoving Laz in passing. He chuckled and lifted his head but didn't pull away from Journey. He never hesitated to kiss her in public, and he did it even more now that he and his beautiful wife were married.

They hadn't planned on eloping, but during a trip to Ocho Rios, Jamaica a couple of months ago, that's what they ended up doing. Journey hadn't wanted a large wedding, and

Laz loved her so much, he would've married her anytime and anywhere. They were married three days into their Jamaica trip.

"Can we eat the cupcakes now?" Dominic asked from behind them.

Laz turned to him. "We need to see if it's okay with—"

"Actually, I was just coming over to suggest we go ahead and find out the gender of Baby Dimas," Geneva said. "All right everyone, gather around. It's time."

Dominic reached for a cupcake. "Wait, Dom," Dakota said as she approached the table. "Let Aunt Jay and Uncle Laz go first." He sighed loudly but stepped back.

"Okay, so is there some type of ritual or…what do we have to do?" Laz glanced at his sister-in-law and Dakota for instructions, but before they could respond, the doorbell rang.

"Wait. Don't do anything. Let me see who that is." Geneva hurried to the door and returned seconds later. "Laz, someone just dropped this off for you."

He read the small card attached to the top of the box and smiled, then glanced at Journey. "This is from Wiz. We're supposed to open it together."

"Hold up. Were we supposed to bring gifts?" Kenton asked, and by the look on everyone's face, they wondered the same thing.

"No, not at all. We just wanted to find out our baby's gender with our friends and family around us," Journey said.

"But when I throw them a baby shower, I expect you to bring a gift," Geneva said.

Kenton shook his head and put his hands up. "I don't do baby showers, but I'll send a gift." Several of the men in the room voiced their agreement.

Dakota put her hands on her hips and scowled. "Well, considering how you wimps are grumbling, I guess we won't be throwing a co-ed baby shower."

"Here, come and sit down," Laz said to Journey, pointing to an upholstered chair in the attached family room.

After she was sitting, he sat on the arm of the chair and handed her the box. "You open it."

"Does that mean you already know what it is?" she asked, ripping off the wrapping paper and finding a smaller box inside of the larger one.

"I have an idea, but I'm not positive."

"Oh my, this is beautiful," she said pulling out a platinum watch with small diamonds around the face. "I don't understand. Why would Wiz send me a watch?"

"There's probably a note," Hamilton said. Everyone was standing around watching them.

Journey dug around inside the large box and found one. "It's addressed to you," she said to Laz.

He quickly read it and smiled.

"What does it say, Uncle Laz?" Dominic asked, sitting on the other side of Journey.

"It says: *Laz, here's a little something to help keep up with your woman, and when your daughter is old enough, we'll outfit her with a bracelet.*"

Journey frowned. "I don't understand."

"There's a tracking device inside the watch. So, if any assho…" Laz started but stopped, and glanced at Dominic, who was grinning.

"You said a swear word again, but I know you can't help it," Dominic said seriously, causing those in the room to laugh.

"Anyway," Laz continued, "If anything should happen to you, the GPS in there will help me find you, no matter where you are."

"I'm not sure how I feel about you knowing my every move," Journey said, but eventually smiled. "But I'll be wearing this every day."

Laz accepted the sweet kiss from her. He hadn't known when Wiz would send the jewelry and had been concerned that Journey wouldn't want to wear it.

"Wait a minute," Journey said. "What makes him think we're having a girl?"

"I was wondering the same thing," Geneva and Dakota said, with Egypt standing next to them nodding. Everyone started talking at once, some saying they'd caught that, while others wanted to see the note.

"Okay, I might've told him that we were having a girl," Laz admitted.

"You don't even know what we're having. How…" Journey paused and glared at him. "I can't believe you!" She swatted his arm. "You already know, don't you?"

"I couldn't help it. I wanted to know. I'm not as patient as you are."

"I can't believe you went behind my back and found out," Journey complained, shaking her head. After feigning annoyance, tears filled her eyes, and a slow smile lit up her face. "We're having a little girl," she whispered in awe, cupping his cheek with her hand. "Are you okay with that?"

Laz turned his head slightly and kissed her palm. "I'm better than okay with that, baby." He didn't care if it was a boy or a girl as long as Journey and the baby were healthy.

"But I don't want a godsister," Dominic chimed in, folding his arms across his chest and looking as if someone told him Christmas was canceled this year.

"What's wrong with having a godsister?" Laz asked.

"Because Dee said I have to share my treehouse with my godbrother or my godsister. I don't want no girl in it. She's going to mess it up and put stupid dolls in it," he said with disgust.

"Man, you don't have to worry about that," Laz assured, squeezing Dominic's shoulder. "My daughter is going to be into basketball, trucks, and water guns. She won't—"

"Laz!" Journey glared at him. "Why would you tell him that?"

"What? It's true."

"Cool!" Dominic pumped his fist in the air. "Then she can hang out with me and my little brother."

"You don't have a brother, sweetheart," Journey said, still scowling at Laz.

"But I'm getting a broth..." Dominic stopped suddenly, a look of terror on his face as he glanced at his parents. "Oops...sorry."

All eyes turned to Hamilton and Dakota.

"Something you guys want to tell us?" Laz asked, amused by his friend's expression. Clearly, Dominic wasn't supposed to say anything.

"There's not much to tell since a certain somebody can't keep a secret." Hamilton shook his head, but Laz didn't miss the excitement on his and Dakota's faces.

"We didn't want to infringe on your celebration, but...we're having a baby...a boy!" Dakota squealed.

Cheers and congratulations went up around the room, and Laz couldn't have been happier for his friends. The best part was that their kids would grow up together.

An hour later after most of their guests had left, Laz walked up behind Journey and wrapped his arms around her, his hands resting on her baby bump. "You doing okay?"

"I'm great," she said turning in his arms to face him. "You have to admit that the party was wonderful."

"I'll admit, I had a great time, but that's always the case when I'm with you."

"I feel the same way, and soon it will be the three of us. I'm beyond excited for this next step in our lives."

"Me too, baby. It's only going to get better from here."

There were still moments when Laz had a hard time believing his good fortune that Journey was in his life, and he looked forward to seeing what else was in store for them.

*

If you enjoyed this book by Sharon C. Cooper, consider leaving a review on any online book site, review site or social media outlet.

Join Sharon's Mailing List

To get sneak peeks of upcoming stories and to hear about giveaways that Sharon is sponsoring, go to **https://bit.ly/1Sih6ol** to join her mailing list.

About the Author

Award-winning and bestselling author, Sharon C. Cooper, is a romance-a-holic - loving anything that involves romance with a happily-ever-after, whether in books, movies, or real life. Sharon writes contemporary romance, as well as romantic suspense and enjoys rainy days, carpet picnics, and peanut butter and jelly sandwiches. She's been nominated for numerous awards and is the recipient of an Emma Award for Romantic Suspense of the Year 2015 (Truth or Consequences), Emma Award - Interracial Romance of the Year 2015 (All You'll Ever Need), and BRAB (book club) Award -Breakout Author of the Year 2014. When Sharon is not writing or working, she's hanging out with her amazing husband, doing volunteer work or reading a good book (a romance of course). To read more about Sharon and her novels, visit www.sharoncooper.net

Connect with Sharon Online:

Website: http://sharoncooper.net

Facebook:
http://www.facebook.com/AuthorSharonCCooper21?ref=hl

Twitter: https://twitter.com/#!/Sharon_Cooper1
Subscribe to her blog: http://sharonccooper.wordpress.com/

Goodreads:
http://www.goodreads.com/author/show/5823574.Sharon_C_Cooper

Pinterest: https://www.pinterest.com/sharonccooper/

Other Titles

Atlanta's Finest Series
Vindicated (book 1)
Indebted (book 2)
Accused (book 3) – coming soon

Jenkins & Sons Construction Series (Contemporary Romance)
Love Under Contract
Proposal for Love

Jenkins Family Series (Contemporary Romance)
Best Woman for the Job (Short Story Prequel)
Still the Best Woman for the Job (book 1)
All You'll Ever Need (book 2)
Tempting the Artist (book 3)
Negotiating for Love (book 4)
Seducing the Boss Lady (book 5)
Love at Last (Holiday Novella)
When Love Calls (Novella)

Reunited Series (Romantic Suspense)
Blue Roses (book 1)
Secret Rendezvous (Prequel to Rendezvous with Danger)
Rendezvous with Danger (book 2)
Truth or Consequences (book 3)
Operation Midnight (book 4)

Stand Alones
Something New ("Edgy" Sweet Romance)
Legal Seduction (Harlequin Kimani – Contemporary Romance)
Sin City Temptation (Harlequin Kimani – Contemporary Romance)

A Dose of Passion (Harlequin Kimani – Contemporary Romance)
Model Attraction (Harlequin Kimani – Contemporary Romance)
A Passionate Kiss (Bennett Triplets Series)

Made in the USA
Middletown, DE
16 April 2022